PENGUIN BOOKS

FRESH FROM THE COUNTRY

Miss Read, or in real life Mrs Dora Saint, is a teacher by profession who started writing after the Second World War, beginning with light essays written for *Punch* and other journals. She has written on educational and country matters, and worked as a script-writer for the B.B.C.

Miss Read is married to a retired schoolmaster and they have one daughter. They live in a tiny Berkshire hamlet. She is a local magistrate and her hobbies are theatre-going, listening to music and reading.

Miss Read has published numerous books, including *Village School* (1955), *Village Diary* (1957), *Storm in the Village* (1958), *Thrush Green* (1959), *Winter in Thrush Green* (1961), an anthology, *Country Bunch* (1963), *Over the Gate* (1964), *The Market Square* (1966), *Village Christmas* (1966), *The Howards of Caxley* (1967), *The Fairacre Festival* (1968), *News from Thrush Green* (1970), *Tyler's Row* (1972), *The Christmas Mouse* (1973), *Farther Afield* (1974), *Battles at Thrush Green* (1975), *No Holly for Miss Quinn* (1976), *Village Affairs* (1977), *Return to Thrush Green* (1978), *The White Robin* (1979), *Village Centenary* (1980), *Gossip from Thrush Green* (1981), *Affairs at Thrush Green* (1983), *Summer at Fairacre* (1984), *At Home in Thrush Green* (1985) and *The School at Thrush Green* (1987). Many of Miss Read's books are published in Penguin, together with four omnibus editions: *Chronicles of Fairacre*, *Life at Thrush Green*, *More Stories from Thrush Green* and *Further Chronicles of Fairacre*. She has also written two books for children, *Hobby Horse Cottage* and *Hob and the Horse-Bat*, The Red Bus series for the very young, a cookery book, *Miss Read's Country Cooking*, and two volumes of autobiography, *A Fortunate Grandchild* (1985) and *Time Remembered* (1986).

MISS READ

FRESH FROM THE COUNTRY

ILLUSTRATED BY J. S. GOODALL

PENGUIN BOOKS

in association with Michael Joseph

PENGUIN BOOKS

Published by the Penguin Group
27 Wrights Lane, London W8 5TZ, England
Viking Penguin Inc., 40 West 23rd Street, New York, New York 10010, USA
Penguin Books Australia Ltd, Ringwood, Victoria, Australia
Penguin Books Canada Ltd, 2801 John Street, Markham, Ontario, Canada L3R 1B4
Penguin Books (NZ) Ltd, 182–190 Wairau Road, Auckland 10, New Zealand

Penguin Books Ltd, Registered Offices: Harmondsworth, Middlesex, England

First published by Michael Joseph 1960
Published in Penguin Books 1962
10

Printed and bound in Great Britain by
Cox & Wyman Ltd, Reading
Typeset in Garamond

To Lil with love

CONTENTS

PART ONE
Transplanted

PART TWO
Finding Roots

PART THREE
New Growth

One place suits one person, another place suits another person. For my part I prefer to live in the country, like Timmy Willie.

BEATRIX POTTER
The Tale of Johnny Town-Mouse

PART ONE

Transplanted

1. Country Beginnings

'And baths extra, of course,' said Mrs Flynn.

She crossed the diminutive landing in four steps and hurled herself against the bathroom door. It creaked, as if in protest, but remained closed.

'All our doors,' gasped Mrs Flynn, getting her shoulder to it, 'are well-fitting.' At the third shove the door groaned open and Anna Lacey peered over her prospective landlady's shoulder into a white-tiled cube of a room which reminded her of the small recess in the dairy at her farmhouse home where two milk churns habitually stood.

'It looks very nice,' said Anna politely. One of the frosted glass windows, studded with perpetual raindrops, was open, and through the chink she caught a glimpse of half-finished houses in another road on the new estate.

Mrs Flynn flicked a speck of dust from the green plastic towel rail and adjusted a mauve bath-mat, sprigged coyly with violets, which hung over the edge of the bath.

'And now I'll take you to the bedroom,' said Mrs Flynn, edging sideways past the girl and taking another four steps across the landing to an open door. She spoke, thought Anna, as though she were about to embark on a lengthy traversal of corridors and staircases rather than this shifting from one foot to the other in order to get from one room to the next in this doll-size house. Used as she was to the big shabby farmhouse on the Suffolk–Essex border, the toy-like dimensions of Mrs Flynn's establishment both fascinated and depressed her.

'This would be *all yours*,' Mrs Flynn announced, waving her hand, with a spacious gesture, at a strip of a room which was roughly the size of the broom-cupboard at Anna's home. The girl looked at it in wonder.

A narrow bed, covered with a fawn folk-weave bedspread, lay close against the wall behind the door. There was one small window placed high, directly below the eaves of the house, and under this stood a prim cane-bottomed chair. The only other piece of furniture was a small chest of drawers round which Mrs Flynn edged towards a cretonne curtain hanging across the corner of the room.

'And here's your wardrobe,' she said proudly. She twitched the curtain aside to show a rail containing three yellow wooden coat hangers. 'You've probably got hangers of your own,' added Mrs Flynn, looking suddenly anxious.

'Oh yes, indeed,' said Anna hastily. 'I could bring my own hangers.'

Despite the July sunshine the room seemed cold and dark, but the red patterned lino was well polished and the thin rug was clean. With a few of my own things about, thought Anna, it might not look so bleak.

She pressed back against the wall to allow Mrs Flynn to pass, and followed her downstairs. The sitting-room door was as stubborn as the bathroom one, the new wood protesting as Mrs Flynn forced it to give way.

She motioned Anna towards a small plump couch, which rested upon skittish surprised wooden legs, and seated herself in a chair which matched it. The room was sparsely furnished. Four pale pictures of pink and blue birds in flowery branches hung, one on each cream wall, very high up near the picture rail.

'From my *Woman's Monthly*,' said Mrs Flynn following the girl's gaze. 'And my nephew Ray passypartooed them.'

Anna switched her gaze to the tiled mantelpiece where a young man's photograph stood. He looked an unprepossessing youth in R.A.F. uniform, and glowered beneath a bar of black brows. His aunt's sharp little face had softened as she surveyed the boy, but now she turned abruptly to Anna and became her business-like self again.

'Three pounds a week is my charge,' said Mrs Flynn, 'and, as I said, baths extra.'

'I should be going home at the weekend – ' began Anna shyly.

'I'm afraid I couldn't make any reduction for that,' Mrs Flynn said, with a wintry smile. 'Not with the overheads.'

'I suppose not,' murmured Anna, wondering just exactly what overheads might be.

'You'd have your main meal at school, I've no doubt,' went on Mrs Flynn, 'and we usually have high tea when Mr Flynn gets in at seven. You probably get a cup of tea at school during the afternoon?' Her voice held a query.

'I'm not sure about that –' Anna began.

'It's usual,' Mrs Flynn assured her swiftly. Anna, who was fond of her food and had the healthy appetite of one just twenty, wryly watched her meals being whittled away by Mrs Flynn's sharp business methods. She felt that she was no match for this woman, but knew that the headmistress's words to her an hour ago were true.

'Digs in this neighbourhood are few and far between. If Mrs Flynn can't take you you will have to face a bus journey each day. I'd try her for a bit,' she had said, and Anna had recognized the soundness of the case.

'I'll know more about that when I start next term,' said Anna. She was pleasantly surprised to hear how firmly this remark had come forth, and, much emboldered, she followed up her small advantage.

'I should need somewhere to work in the evenings. There will be books to mark and handwork to prepare, you know.'

'There's the bedroom,' Mrs Flynn pointed out. She sounded slightly affronted. Anna determined not to give way.

'But I shall need a table.'

'Then I suppose you might have the use of this room occasionally,' said Mrs Flynn somewhat grudgingly. 'It would be a little more of course. I hadn't bargained for letting two rooms.

In fact, I think I shall have to speak to Mr Flynn before decid-
ing about that.'

What a useful thing a husband must be, thought Anna! She
looked at the clock on the mantelpiece. It was an impressive
object made of black marble in the form of a Greek temple. It
began a preliminary whirring before striking three o'clock.

The girl remembered her long journey back to north Essex,
collected her gloves and bag, and rose to her feet.

'I'm sure we shall be able to come to some arrangement
about using this room,' Mrs Flynn said hastily, in a slightly
more conciliatory tone, as she saw her prey escaping. 'But, you
see, I must have somewhere to bring friends, and when Ray's
here he likes somewhere to play his guitar.'

'Perhaps just one or two evenings a week it might be possible for me to use it,' suggested Anna. 'In any case, I'll think
it over and let you know before the end of the week.'

Mrs Flynn jerked open the door and led the way to the front
door.

'Holiday times,' she said, as she opened it, 'there would be a
retention fee of ten shillings.'

'Oh yes,' said Anna, a little bewildered. 'Ten shillings for
each holiday?'

'Ten shillings a week!' Mrs Flynn answered, with a hint of
triumph. 'It's quite usual.'

'I'll remember,' said Anna.

Mrs Flynn accompanied her down the tiny tiled path to the
gate. Under the hot July sun six young golden privet bushes
were struggling for existence in the dusty new front garden,
and a forlorn stick of a lilac bush drooped by the gatepost, its
tag still fluttering from one twig.

'We should have a really nice hedge this time next year,'
observed Mrs Flynn looking fondly at the privet.

'I'm sure you will,' agreed Anna bravely. And on this note
of hope they parted.

Anna's spirits rose as she approached her home. The journey took over two hours from the new raw suburb where she was to take up her teaching appointment next September. She had travelled across the vast sprawling mass of London which sweltered in the throbbing heat and had felt the oppression of spirits which row upon row of streets always produced in her.

As the streets gave way to leafy suburbs and then to the gentle flat country of her own neighbourhood, happiness returned. The wind blew refreshingly through the open window of the Green Line coach, fragrant with the smell of freshly-cut hay and the flowers of many a sunny meadow.

The coach breasted a slight incline and Anna looked with love at the familiar view spread before her. Clumps of elms, blue-green with dense masses of leaves, made dark pools of shade among the wide pale fields of rural Essex. Away to the east the gentle blue of a cloudless sky met the darker blue of the horizon, and beyond that the North Sea heaved and murmured, tossing a lacy froth of shallow waves along the broad sands.

Westward, where Anna's farm lay, little streams made their leisurely way to greater water courses seeking the sea. Willows lined their banks, their silvery leaves shimmering in ceaseless quivering. To Anna, now waiting at the coach door ready to descend at her cross-roads, they seemed to be fluttering in welcome.

The Land Rover was waiting in the shady lane, her mother at the wheel. Anna bounded towards her, eager to tell her of all that had befallen.

Margaret Lacey, Anna's mother, was now approaching fifty, but her energy and youthful looks were the envy of many younger women.

She had been born just before the outbreak of the First World War within a dozen miles of her present home. Her father had been a miller and had lived and worked all his life in the tall lovely building which stood by the waters of the river Low. The sound of the rushing mill race was the background music to her happy upbringing, so much so that when she went to stay elsewhere she would lie awake at night missing the voice of those tumbling waters which normally hushed her to sleep.

She was the youngest of four children. Her father, James North, a burly, red-faced giant of a man, had brought up his two boys and two girls to lead as energetic a life as his own. His wife had been of gentler stuff, and although she baked and mended and ran her boisterous household with method and cheerfulness, there was a quality of secret reserve about her which her family recognized but, with the exception of Margaret, did not understand.

Poetry she loved and the wild flowers and animal life of the countryside. Limp-backed editions of Browning and Tennyson lay beside her bed and in her gleaming drawing-room. Bowls of primroses scented the air in spring, and the tang of autumn was carried into the house with the great sprays of tawny leaves which she bore home from her solitary walks. More often than not some small wounded creature, a bird with a broken wing or a nestful of baby field-mice orphaned by the hay-cutter, would be receiving care and hospitality in the great kitchen, and Margaret shared her mother's compassion, treating the rest of the family's good-natured teasing with the same unsentimental charity which characterized all her mother's actions.

Margaret had cycled with her brothers and sister into the market town six miles away for her schooling, and, that over, had worked at the council offices there overlooking the wide river which earlier in its course had splashed past her mill home.

She had entered into the life of the friendly little town, acting in the Dramatic Club's plays, playing tennis, and boating with other young people, but still in her dinner hours she would go into the library near by or the local bookshop and find her way to the shelves where the modern poets could be found, a secret joy which was to endure through her whole life.

She had known Patrick Lacey and his family from her schooldays. He was a hefty, good-tempered young man, a stalwart forward in the local rugby team and a welcome addition to any party in the neighbourhood. His father farmed within a few miles of Margaret's home and he too worked there and would eventually take it over.

He and Margaret slipped into marriage naturally and happily, after a brief courtship notable for its complete lack of lovers' quarrels. They had set up house in a cottage on the farm, but within six months Patrick's father had died and the young couple moved into the farmhouse.

And it was here, one snowy morning during the following winter, that Margaret's first child, Anna, was born.

She had been a happy child, with her father's good-nature and fair good looks, and the births of her two younger brothers caused her no undue jealousy.

Her upbringing was as practical and sensible as her mother's and father's had been. She early learnt the simple virtues of truthfulness and neighbourliness, prized perhaps more keenly in a place where all one's past was an open book, and encouraged in the low church of St Jude's where the family worshipped regularly every Sunday morning.

She had grown into a straight-backed, long-legged girl with a mop of fair curly hair which defied any of Anna's attempts to wean it from its natural exuberance to more sleek and modish styles. She had cycled, as her mother had done, the few miles to the same school and had been taught by several of those teachers who had taught her mother too. Her academic ability was average, her disposition patient and cheerful, her health boisterous. Her pleasure in children's company extended even to that of her vociferous young brothers! It was no wonder that she was advised to take up teaching by her headmistress.

Margaret too was pleased when Anna decided to accept the advice and had filled in her forms for admission to a training college for teachers. Firstly, she wanted her to be happy and to be engaged in work which she was capable of doing with zest and efficiency. Secondly, she wanted the girl to do something useful in the world. Her own family and her husband's had been brought up in the tradition of useful service to those among whom they lived. 'Using one's talents' was the theme of many a sermon by their present vicar, and it chimed with their own feelings and experience.

Both these reasons she spoke of to Anna and to her husband. Patrick, as is the way with fathers, was very content to leave the arrangements to his women-folk, but was wholeheartedly in favour of Anna's choice and generous in his financial proposals to the girl.

'It's a good training,' was his verdict. 'Working with children will stand you in good stead if you have a family of your own, and if you don't – well, other people's children are the next best thing. What's more,' he added, with practical wisdom, 'you can earn a living wherever you choose to go in the world, and have a pension at the end of it! Which is more than I shall.' He had ruffled his daughter's yellow hair, and gone out, whistling, to feed the pigs. For him, the matter was comfortably settled.

To Margaret this prosaic assessment of the decision was only part of the matter.

There was another reason for her pleasure in Anna's choice which Margaret had not mentioned to her husband. It would mean that she would have a few more years at her studies and that the love of books and poetry which meant so much, and to which she could afford to give so little time, in her own busy everyday existence, would be fostered in Anna.

For Margaret believed that the love was there but not yet fully awakened. So far, in Anna's eighteen years, the healthy open-air life of the farm, riding with her brothers, playing games with her friends and relishing all the joys that the windy wide meadows and the glittering river offered, had filled the girl's time. But, as Margaret knew, there were things of the mind which could offer a more powerful refreshment of the spirit. As the years passed she had found the distillation of men's experience, the essence of their emotions and beliefs in prose or poetry, a source of inner strength and comfort.

The second commandment, 'To love thy neighbour as thyself,' was the everyday standard which the family had set itself and which, by dint of good fellowship, pleasant circumstances, an unhurried way of life and a genuine warm-hearted interest in those around them, it was comparatively easy to keep. It was a rule-of-thumb code of behaviour which could carry a man successfully through a lifetime. But Margaret knew that it was not enough.

She realized that 'the first and great commandment' held the key to essential happiness. To recognize absolute goodness and absolute truth translated in terms of fine music, painting, or poetry, was to feel that answering, powerful, thrilling rightness which one knew one shared with mankind the world over. It was this mercurial leap of the spirit to something above and beyond it which Margaret wanted her daughter to know, the incandescent flash caused by the fusion of two minds, albeit centuries apart.

Without it, Anna could live the useful, happy life her father envisaged. But with it, her mother knew, 'something rich and strange' would weave its unalloyed gold thread through the serviceable homespun of her working days.

During the early part of the evening, after Anna had told her mother of the afternoon's happenings, the girl wandered through the garden to a leafy lane near by.

The air was very still. Far away she could hear the sound of her father's baler clack-clacking in a distant hay-field. She leaned upon a gate and looked at the wheat spreading acre

after acre before her. It was sturdy and green, and the girl realized, with a start, that by the time it had turned golden she would be teaching, and would not be there to see all the days of harvest.

For the first time, she had doubts. The great new primary school, flashing with glass, the rows and rows of little tables in each classroom for the infants and juniors, and the formidably long queues of children traversing the endless corridors had daunted her. It was unlike any of the schools she had met before, either during school practice at college or in the rural neighbourhood of her home county.

The building, she admitted, was magnificent. Never had she seen such lightness, such colour, such gleaming expanses of floor and such flashing rows of wash-basins. Around this palace had stretched ten acres of grass beyond the immaculate asphalt area which would have served many schools as their only playground.

And yet the place had depressed her. She remembered the string of new factories which she had passed on her way there that afternoon. The school was not unlike them at first sight, massive, immaculate, teeming with life, and yet impersonal. She remembered the square red-brick school which she herself had attended, its comfortable domestic outline shrouded in homely creeper. Here two hundred girls had worked and played and had thought themselves a large body of people. How would she fare with six hundred under one roof?

Ah well, thought Anna philosophically, plucking a sprig of honeysuckle and smelling it while she could, there were all the summer holidays before her. The great school, the ugly raw new estate, and Mrs Flynn were a long way ahead.

Meanwhile all the joys of home and summer thronged about her. The whinny of her pony in the paddock lifted her spirits, and retracing her steps Anna made her way back to the home which, to her surprise, suddenly seemed doubly dear.

As she emerged from the leafy tunnel of the lane the sound of the hay-baler came more clearly, thumping out its cheerful noise across the golden evening fields.

'Make hay while the sun shines,' quoted Anna aloud. It seemed as encouraging a proverb as any under the circumstances, and much comforted, she ran up the flagged path and into the open door.

2. Morning at Elm Hill

THE golden days slipped by all too swiftly and on the second day of September Anna crossed the playground to start her first day's teaching.

She had spent a wakeful night in the narrow bed under Mrs Flynn's roof. The mattress had seemed uncommonly thin and hard after the engulfing softness of the feather-beds of home, but it was not only that which had kept sleep at bay. The thought of what the morrow might hold had kept her mind active. Would she be able to keep order? Would the children be ready to listen and willing to learn? For that matter, did she honestly know anything to teach them? And if so, could she impart it?

She had tried to remember her college lectures and the criticisms she had received during school practice in the ancient cathedral city in which the college had stood. But coherent thought eluded her. Her mind slipped about, turning and twisting like a fish in tumultuous waters. Jumbled images of the half-forgotten faces of fellow-students, the swinging clapper of the college bell above the great gate, and the musty half-light of the crowded college chapel swam before her, and that was all.

At last, as the first lorries began to drone their way along the main road near by, she had fallen into a deep sleep which was soon shattered by the alarm clock beside her.

She had eaten her first breakfast at Mrs Flynn's in a daze, had scrutinized her reflection in the little mirror in her bedroom and decided that the flowered cotton frock and white sandals were suitable for her first appearance in public, and had gone forth, inwardly quaking, to meet the day.

And now, as she crossed the playground, she was conscious of a dozen young eyes upon her. The first few children paused in their play, and followed her progress with silent curiosity. It was very early, barely half past eight, and the school bell would not summon the children until ten to nine, but Anna was anxious to get into her classroom and see to her preparations.

She made her way first to the headmistress's room upstairs, trying to remember, as she mounted the shallow stone steps, the geography of the school from her quick and bemused tour of it on that July afternoon.

This primary school had two floors, she knew, the infants, aged five to seven, being housed on the ground floor, and the junior children, of seven to eleven, on the first. The building was a hollow square round a quadrangle, which was attractive with mown grass and bright flower-beds. The east and south sides were given over to classrooms, five below for infants and five above for the older children. On the north side lay the cloakrooms and the cleaners' cupboards and storerooms on the ground floor, and above them the staff rooms and capacious stock rooms holding books, stationery, and all the paraphernalia of school life; while the west side of the square was entirely taken up by a lofty hall, with a stage at one end, and a green room beyond it.

Anna reached the landing, tiptoed past a door marked STAFF CLOAKROOM and approached a distant one bearing a neat label encased in a brass frame. It said:

HEADMISTRESS
(MISS F. R. ENDERBY)

It was unnaturally quiet in the empty corridor. Anna was conscious of the clean smell of furniture polish and carbolic soap mingled together, an ineffable emanation from the woodwork and stone of the great building, which she was to recognize all through her life as the very essence of first-day-of-term in any school throughout the land.

She knocked timidly upon the pale polished wood of the door just below the brass frame and stood back to wait. Silence engulfed her again. She read the directions on a bright red fire extinguisher with an intentness born of extreme nervous tension and wiped her damp palms with a crumpled handkerchief.

A faint measured clicking sound reached her straining ears, and she realized that it was the ticking of the electric clocks each watching over a classroom with a bland indifferent face. Somewhere, far below, a door banged and a child squealed, breaking the spell of near-panic which bound the girl. She moved away from the cold corrugation of the radiator against which she had been pressing herself and approached the door again, swallowing painfully to relieve the constriction of her throat.

This time she knocked more loudly, and before the noise had died away into the implacable, waiting emptiness of the vast building, she had her answer.

'Come in!' echoed very faintly from within and, grasping the cold oval handle in her sweaty palm, Anna prepared to meet her headmistress.

Florence Rhoda Enderby was a handsome large woman in her late forties. Her white hair was cut short and waved becomingly above her square brown face. Dark eyes, under strongly-marked brows, added to her air of lively intelligence. She dressed with taste and care, and her attractive appearance did much to impress both pupils and their parents with her general capability.

A large square-cut sapphire on the ring finger of her left hand, about which she was mysteriously reticent, also added a touch of glamour and pathos. It was generally supposed, from the few clues which she had dropped and from the clouding of her fine eyes when she surveyed the ring, that her fiancé had been killed whilst flying during the last war. Anna was to learn more of this mystery later.

She had been appointed the first headmistress of Elm Hill School when it had opened three years earlier and had already received praise for work well done there. Before her present appointment she had taught, first as an assistant near Wolverhampton, the town of her birth, and later as the headmistress of a small infant and junior school in the same area. Her appointment to Elm Hill had caused some chagrin among local teachers who had hoped for this plum to be plucked by one of their number, but resentment towards the newcomer had soon died down and she was generally admitted to be making a good job of it.

The school had been built for three hundred and fifty children, but within eighteen months was housing over five hundred. Now, at the beginning of its fourth school year, almost six hundred children were crammed into the majestic building.

The ten classrooms which were to have held less than forty children apiece, were now a tight mass of desks, wedged so closely together that it was difficult to move up and down the meagre gangways left between the rows. The numbers were nearer fifty than forty in each class, and the spacious hall which had so delighted the new headmistress and her staff now housed two more classes.

Here, where Florence Enderby had had such high hopes of staging frequent plays, of daily dancing sessions, of physical training periods in wet weather, and of ample room for a dozen communal activities, stood tables and chairs for eighty infants. One class faced the stage, the other the back of the hall, and two much-tried teachers pitted their voices against each other and grew daily nearer dementia as they watched the back row of their own class twisting round to attend to the lesson going on at the other end of the hall.

The green room too had been commandeered. Here there was only room for a very small class and eighteen backward juniors lived amid a welter of tidy-boxes, educational apparatus, glove-puppets, half-finished models of farmyards, railway stations, and the like, as well as a large table map of the immediate vicinity of Elm Hill School complete with model lorries, tankers, and cars much too big for the crayoned roads.

And now this term, the last free space had gone. Two staff rooms flanked Miss Enderby's apartment, one labelled

STAFF
(MISTRESSES)

a large airy room, and the other, with

STAFF
(MASTERS)

on the door, a smaller establishment. It was this latter room which had been furnished as another classroom, and here that twenty children, just risen from the infant department downstairs to the dizzy height of first-year juniors upstairs, would have their lessons.

The masters were to share the same staff room as the women on the staff, but as there were only four males to add to the ten females normally using it there would be plenty of room.

There was no doubt about it, Florence Enderby had been telling herself just before Anna had knocked, the new building was already overdue. Work was to begin some time this term on an entirely separate school, but in the same grounds, which was to be solely for infants, while Elm Hill would remain as the junior department.

'And the sooner the better,' thought the headmistress, looking out of her window upon the playground which was growing uncomfortably full as ten to nine approached. Her thoughts turned, as they had so often done lately, to the headship of the new establishment and that of her present school. She had no doubt that a man would be appointed in her place in the fullness of time. The infant school headship might well be hers if she applied for it. Certainly a headship somewhere near by would be offered her, but at the moment Florence Enderby was not sure of her plans.

She was an ambitious woman and she intended to get on. Already she was known as the 'Manners-Maniac' among her critics, for she insisted on punctilious courtesy at all times in her school, sometimes carrying it to such excessive lengths that it bordered on the ridiculous. The Elm Hill children were known by their old-fashioned courtliness which could be both charming and exasperating.

She had certainly made her mark upon the place already. She was a born organizer and adept at creating order from chaos. Forms, statistics, and questionnaires were a joy to her and new theories and methods in education she found engrossing and challenging. Her capabilities seemed to match her competent and pleasing appearance. Here, people said, is surely the perfect headmistress!

Only in one respect did Florence Enderby fail. Although she hardly realized it herself and would have denied it strenuously if she had been told, the fact remained, Florence Enderby did not like children.

She recognized that they were essential to her job. They were the raw material upon which her skill could work and upon whom new methods could be tried and results noted.

She was proud to see them, hundreds of them, in neat rows in the hall at morning assembly, answering her greeting with their shrill light voices accompanied by those curtsies from the girls and bows from the boys which so many of her staff deprecated as 'olde-worlde' and distinctly bad for their headmistress's ego which they felt was already too confidently established.

She liked too to see them at play on the wide green expanse of grass about the school, scampering and fluttering in their bright clothes, bringing colour and gaiety to the raw open neighbourhood as yet unbeautified with trees and mellowed

gardens. They were her school, her children, the living evidence of her work and effort. Collectively she gloried in them. As individuals she found them tiresome.

This morning as she gazed down upon them arriving thick and fast in the playground, the feeling of pride was dominant. A school of nearly six hundred! she told herself triumphantly. She had done well. She had never thought, when she had started on her career almost thirty years before, that such a headship would ever be hers! She had come a long way from the grimy Victorian building in Wolverhampton where she had faced her first class. She believed that she might find further glories before she finally retired from the field after forty years' service, and the vision of the new infants' school glowed brightly before her inward eye. It would be the culmination of a lifetime's teaching.

Anna's light knock at the door put an end to these dreams of the future and brought her abruptly back to the present.

'Come in,' she called in the sonorously flat Midland tones she had never quite lost.

The door opened and, for a brief moment, the headmistress felt herself thirty years back in time. Just so had she stood once, nervous and defenceless, on the threshold of her career, as young and as bewildered as the girl who hesitated in the doorway.

'Don't be afraid,' said Miss Enderby, suddenly compassionate. She advanced across the room, regaining her usual official poise as she came nearer the girl. Her warm smile thawed Anna's chill forebodings as much as the words which followed it.

'I'll take you to meet your class and, I promise you, you'll like each other. This way, my dear.'

Together the old teacher and the young made their way towards Anna's classroom whilst the clanging of a distant bell brought sudden peace to the hubbub in the playground.

'School's begun!' said Anna's headmistress.

3. Anna Meets Her Class

WHILE Anna prepared herself to meet her class of forty-six exuberant and inquisitive children her landlady was busy preparing the high tea for her husband and the new lodger.

She had screwed the ancient mincer to the kitchen table and now fed it with rather tough strips of beef, the remains of the Sunday joint. There was not very much, to be sure, but Mrs Flynn's pinch-penny spirit had been roused to meet this challenge and the heel of a brown loaf, a large onion, and a tomato on the table were ominous portents of the rest of the proposed cottage pie.

'If I open a tin of baked beans,' said Mrs Flynn aloud, 'there'll be no need for gravy. No call to waste gas unnecessarily!' She pursed her thin lips with satisfaction, remembering, with sudden pleasure, that she had purchased the beans at a reduced price as 'THIS WEEK'S AMAZING OFFER' at the local grocer's. She twirled the handle of the mincer with added zest.

Yesterday's stewed apple, she thought busily, could be eked out with a little evaporated milk, and arranged in three individual dishes. A cherry on top of each would make a nice festive touch, decided Mrs Flynn in a wild burst of extravagance. She straightened up from her mincing and opened the store cupboard where she kept her tinned and bottled food. In the front row a small jar of cherries gleamed rosily. For one long minute Mrs Flynn studied its charms, torn between the opposing forces of art and thrift. Victory was accomplished easily.

'Pity to open them,' said Mrs Flynn, slamming the cupboard door, and returned, spiritually purged, to her mincing.

Anna watched her class file in a ragged two-by-two column

through the doorway of her classroom. Miss Enderby, large and imposing, a professionally bright smile curving her mouth, stood beside her and kept up a brisk flow of directions.

'Choose any desks, dears. Yes, you may sit by Bobby if you can behave yourself, Arnold. No, I don't want to see birthday cards now, dear. Nor dinner money. Nor your tortoise's egg. Put it on the window-sill, dear, in the cool.'

She clapped her hands with a sudden deafening report, making Anna, and several of the children, start nervously.

'All behind chairs! Quickly now! I want to introduce you to your new teacher.'

There was a noisy shuffling of chairs and an upheaval of those who had already taken their seats and now must struggle from them. Under cover of the confusion Miss Enderby inclined her well-corseted figure sideways towards Anna and whispered:

'This may seem a little formal to you after the advice you had at college for free movement in the classroom and so on, but we must have a little order with these large numbers.'

Anna nodded agreement. To her bewildered senses the scene presented chaos incarnate. Another thunderous clap from Miss Enderby brought some appreciable quietening of the uproar.

'RIGHT behind chairs!' boomed the headmistress. 'And standing on TWO feet! That's better.'

By now an unholy hush had fallen upon the classroom. Outside Anna could hear the whirring of a cement-mixer. It sounded uncomfortably close at hand, and later that morning she realized that it was just below her window and likely to keep up its merry din for most of the term.

The children fixed their eyes unwinkingly upon Anna. Anna gazed back warily, feeling as helpless as a jelly-fish exposed to the proddings of innumerable sharp sticks.

'Now, children,' began Miss Enderby firmly, 'you are very, very lucky this term to have Miss Lacey for your new teacher.'

Anna gave a watery smile. The children's faces were un-moved.

'Miss Lacey,' repeated Miss Enderby with emphasis. 'Can you say that?'

'Miss Lacey,' chorused the class obediently.

'Perhaps you could say "Good morning" to your new teacher?' suggested Miss Enderby with massive archness.

'Good morning, Miss Lacey,' came the polite chorus.

'Good morning, children,' responded Anna in a croak which bore no resemblance to her normal voice.

The civilities over Miss Enderby motioned to the children to take their seats which they accomplished with the same deafening uproar as before. Anna began to wonder if she would ever get used to it or if she would be compelled to stuff cotton-wool in her ears before these mass upheavals and jerk it out when the class had settled.

'I should give out paper and coloured pencils,' said Miss Enderby, 'as soon as you've called the register. Keep them busy, while you're finding your way about the cupboards and so on.'

She gave a swift look round the docile class. There was a straightening of backs and demureness of demeanour which spoke for an awareness of Miss Enderby's disciplinary powers.

'I expect you to help Miss Lacey in *every* way,' said the head-mistress with a slight edge to her voice. 'D'you hear me, Arnold?'

The little boy addressed, who had been crossing and un-crossing his eyes in an unlovely manner for the delectation of his neighbours, looked suitably crest-fallen.

'Watch that boy,' murmured Miss Enderby, in an audible aside. 'Broken home – brother in Borstal – enlarged tonsils – and some rather dreadful habits which the school psychiatrist says are compensatory, but I think are nasty and nothing more!'

Anna looked with fresh interest at Arnold and thought he

looked far too innocent and apple-cheeked to have such a record. But, even as she looked, she saw a fleeting grimace distort his pink face expressing, in no uncertain terms, his scorn of Miss Enderby who was giving her final messages to the new teacher.

'Break at ten-forty-five, dear,' said the headmistress. 'Come straight to the staff room and I will introduce you to those you didn't meet on your first visit, and we will have a cup of tea then. If there's anything that puzzles you, I shall be in my room. Just send a message by one of the children.'

She made her way to the door and waited before it, eyebrows raised as she turned her affronted gaze upon the children. They gazed back in some bewilderment.

'Is *no one* going to remember his manners?' asked Miss Enderby, carefully grammatic.

With a nervous start Anna hastened forward to the door, but was waved back by an undulation of her headmistress's hand, the sapphire ring flashing in the light. Galvanized into action a dozen or more children leapt to their feet knocking over their chairs as they made an ugly rush to open the door. A freckled mite with two skinny red plaits was the first to hurl herself upon the handle and drag open the door. She was rewarded by a gracious smile.

'Thank you, dear, thank you,' said Miss Enderby and sailed majestically into the corridor. A faint sigh of relief rippled round the class as the door was closed behind her, chests deflated, backs slumped, and the forty-six tongues which had so far kept unnaturally silent began to wag cheerfully.

Anna watched this degeneration with some dismay. For all the notice the class was taking of her she might have been non-existent. She remembered, with sudden relief, some advice given her at college to use in just such a situation.

'Stand quite still, be quite calm, and gradually the children will become conscious that you are waiting. Never, never attempt to shout them down.'

With monumental dignity Anna stood her ground waiting for the chattering to subside. But, far from diminishing, the noise grew in volume as conversations became more animated and far-flung. One or two children scrambled from their chairs and crossed the room to see distant friends. Two little boys attacked each other in brisk amity, a group converged upon the tortoise egg on the window-sill while its owner spread-eagled herself over it protectively, squealing with apprehension. The child with the birthday cards was displaying their beauties to an admiring crowd round her desk and carrying on a high-pitched running commentary on the donors. Arnold, Anna noticed with some trepidation, had removed his blue pullover and was busy scrabbling at the back of his shirt, attempting to pull it over his head, in order, it seemed, to show his friends a minute scar on his shoulder-blade.

Amidst mounting chaos Anna remained silent and statu-esque, clinging desperately, but with receding hope, to the dictum of her college mentor. So might a lone rock stand among tempestuous seas, thought Anna grimly, and with as much hope of quelling them. She looked at the electric clock which jerked spasmodically from one minute to the next and decided to let it leap once more before she abandoned hope.

One crumb of comfort, if comfort it could be called, re-mained with her. This was no outburst against her, but simply an ebullience of natural high spirits among themselves. Her presence, she noted wryly, meant nothing at all to them.

A chair fell over, someone yelped with pain, there was a burst of laughter, and Anna saw the clock jump to another minute. Abandoning her dignified immobility Anna advanced into action. She strode to the front desks and clapped her hands with a resonance which rivalled Miss Enderby's own.

'To your desks!' she roared. 'And quickly!'

With a pleasurable shock she saw her words obeyed. There was a scuffling and a scuttling and within a minute order had returned. Refreshed by their break the children turned attentive eyes upon her.

Anna's self-esteem crept back.

'And about time too!' she commented severely to her waiting class.

The morning dragged on. Anna felt as though she had been weeks in the classroom and felt unaccountably exhausted. The thought of break and tea at a quarter to eleven gleamed in the distance.

She had called the children's names and marked her register with care. Fearful lest uproar should break out again she had kept her voice stern and her face unsmiling. She had mispronounced one or two names and quelled the resulting sniggers with her most daunting glances. This was not how she had envisaged meeting her new charges. She had meant to advance with happiness and confidence, as she had been told to do at college, but she felt neither at the moment, and guilty into the bargain.

Two bustling, self-important little girls had given out paper and pencils to the rest and the class settled itself, with only a minor buzzing, to filling its empty sheets with horses, ballerinas, cowboys, and anything else which engaged its attention, leaving Anna free to roam up and down the aisles and to look from the windows upon the windy sunlit wastes of the new suburb which surrounded the school.

It had rained in the night and although the pavements and the old metalled roads had dried there were still long puddles lying in the ruts of the new muddy lanes which criss-crossed the area. From her high window Anna could see how flat the country was. The new houses were being built on what had once been waste marshland, and the glint of a sluggishly-moving stream and pools of standing water reflecting the pale sky, gave a hint of future fogs and floodings.

It could never have been very pretty, decided Anna, resting

her arms on the window-sill. Only a few desiccated elms remained at the side of the distant main road, wearing flamboy-
ant hoardings round the base of their trunks like tawdry
shabby skirts. The few fields which remained stretched, flat
and monotonous, towards the horizon, hedgeless and with
tufts of coarse marsh weed sprouting through the rusty shab-
biness of the dying grass. Only the sky was beautiful. It
arched above the sad wasteland with bright iridescence, and
Anna remembered with amusement a wonderful phrase from
an old copy of *Suggestions for Teachers*. 'Direct the children's
attention,' it had said, 'to the ever-changing panorama of the
heavens.' The stilted primness of this sensible advice had never
failed to please her, and now, tense and worried, the old
charm still worked and had power to cheer and comfort her.

Smilingly obedient to the injunction she looked up at the
sky. Great pillars of white cloud, billowing into fantastic
shapes, moved majestically across the pale blue sky, dwarfing
the insignificant countryside below into an untidy shabby toy-
land of houses, factories, and hoardings spilt haphazard across
the acres of dingy grass and mud. This glimpse of ever-changing but enduring beauty revived Anna's young spirits.

'Bell, miss!' chorused the class joyously, as a shrilling noise
broke the uneasy peace of the classroom.

Pencils clattered into the grooves of the desks, papers were
stuffed inside, and before Anna could give any orders her class
streamed out through the door and were gone.

There seemed nothing for it but to follow their example.
The corridors were full of hastening noisy children, clutching
paper bags with their lunch inside, skipping ropes, balls, and
other impedimenta.

Anna battled her way against the stream and found herself
at last at the staff room.

There were only fourteen members of staff at Elm Hill
School, but the staff room appeared crowded to Anna's timid

eyes. Several of her colleagues she had met already, either during her July visit, or before school began that morning, but now Miss Enderby bore down upon her and took her to the large central table.

Two men scrambled clumsily to their feet and balanced cigarettes carefully across the edge of their saucers.

'This is Alan Foster,' said Miss Enderby, 'who takes the top class here.'

Anna found herself holding the soft podgy hand of a middle-aged man. He wore a dark, shabby suit, creased from the heavy folds of his pear-shaped body, and decorated with cigarette ash. His eyes were moist and kindly behind horn-rimmed spectacles.

'Hope you'll be happy with us,' he wheezed politely. 'I'll get you some tea.'

'And this is Andy Craig,' continued Miss Enderby, 'who is in the classroom next to yours.' Anna wondered if she could detect a faint coolness in her headmistress's tones as the introductions were made.

Andy Craig was a younger man than Alan Foster, a slight jaunty figure dressed in a jacket of rather large dog-tooth check and tightish cavalry twill trousers. His shoes were as glossy as horse-chestnuts and he sported a bloodstone ring on his little finger. A sandy moustache matched his sandy hair and his eyes were startlingly like bottled gooseberries in their soft opaque greenness. Anna felt that she would rather not be alone with Mr Craig for any length of time.

A large, well-corseted figure in a navy-blue costume whom Anna recognized as Miss Hobbs, the second-in-command, now approached Miss Enderby and said importantly:

'A traveller, dear, outside your door. I told him you were engaged and he'd have to wait –'

'I'd better see him,' said Miss Enderby, depositing her half-filled cup on the table. Miss Hobbs's eyes watched her departing figure with concern.

'*Quite* selfless!' she announced in a dramatic aside to Anna. 'The school *always* comes first!' She turned solemn dark eyes upon the girl.

'You just don't know how lucky you are to be serving under Florence Enderby,' she said earnestly. 'She's a really *wonderful* woman!'

At this point a plastic beaker full of steaming tea was thrust between them by the tall young woman Anna had seen standing at the side table busy pouring out.

'Remember me?' she asked. 'Joan Berry? Are you completely exhausted?'

Miss Hobbs, looking a little huffy, moved away to make room for the newcomer and Anna smiled at the elegant Miss Berry whose glamorous appearance had impressed her so much at their first meeting.

'Do you know everyone now?' continued Joan Berry. 'We're all here, I think, except Tom Drew and John Fraser who are on playground duty, and the two moles who've gone to earth again.'

She laughed at Anna's bewilderment, but rattled on.

'You'll have to bring a cup and saucer for yourself. We all do. That's why you had to wait for the beaker.'

'I'll bring one,' promised Anna, making a mental note to go shopping as soon as school was over. Mrs Flynn was not likely to offer such richness to her lodger, Anna thought to herself.

The electric bell shrilled again and Anna, copying her fellows, gulped down the remains of her tea.

'We go down to the playground to see our classes in,' said Miss Berry taking Anna's arm.

'Tell me about the moles –' began Anna as they descended
the stone steps.

'Hush!' whispered her companion. 'Too many ears about
now. But I warn you, my dear, we're a very rum lot at Elm
Hill. Very rum indeed!'

4. Pavements and Parents

THE new streets of Elm Hill, which spread daily further and further across the wasteland, enclosed the old village of that name. All that remained of it was a shabby towered church built of grey flints, a row of cottages of the same stone, a square white vicarage with a slated roof, and a dingy pub.

There had once been a village green, bordered on one side by a row of horse-chestnut trees; and a rough area of grass, bare in patches from many feet, was still to be seen near the pub. Half-a-dozen chestnut trees still stood, their lower branches broken off by the hands of hooligans, and gaps showed where their fellows had been cut down one here, one there, to be taken to the timber yard.

Three families lived in the vicarage, the vicar having only the ground floor for his domain. The garden, shared by all, had that neglected, 'someone-else-can-do-it' look so often found in communal property.

A rusty tricycle and a headless doll lay under the rhododendron bushes. Plantains and daisies starred the shabby lawns, and formal flower beds, which had once glowed with geraniums, lobelias, and roses to delight the eyes of former incumbents whose stipends allowed gardeners, had been grassed over, only their shape showing like pale ghosts against the older sward.

Only the massive cedar retained its dignity. Lofty, superb, its blue-black branches spreading horizontally like massive hands in constant and magnificent blessing, it surveyed both the fading gentility of its own house and the new ugliness which pressed around it. It stood inviolate, like a lone hero who, surrounded by a mob, fears none but pities all.

A mile away lay the railway station and here, almost a

hundred years ago, another village had grown up. The square yellow houses, early grimed with smoke from the trains, still stood, mean and dejected, topped with grey slates. A row of small shops, The Railway Tavern, and two or three detached villas hidden behind grimy laurels were all that remained of the original second village, but over the years the streets had crept between the two, first over the flat fields that bordered the railway and then over the slight rise in the meadows, once crowned with a clump of elm trees, which had given its name to the village.

A gas-lit Post Office, a Working-Men's Institute, more public houses, a British Legion Hall, fish-and-chip shops, temporary churches, a new Broadway built in the mid thirties and flashing as garishly as false teeth in a faded face, were added to the mess which gradually covered the fields.

Anna had explored this sad hinterland, one sunny evening on a solitary walk, soon after her arrival. She had walked half a mile through the new half-made roads among which her lodgings lay and crossed the old turnpike road, busy with homeward-going traffic to the north-west.

She could not decide which was the more depressing, the arid near-slums on one side of the main road or the new chaotic rawness on the other. She had made her way towards the church knowing that the origins of the place would be near by and anxious to see what remained of the village it had once been.

Her spirits had fallen as she walked. There seemed nothing, absolutely nothing, to cheer the heart or delight the eye. Even the 'ever-changing panorama of the heavens' was unremarkable that evening.

She had stopped at the vicarage gate, arrested by the sight of the one splendid cedar tree. In her present mood it only seemed to emphasize the pitifulness of its surroundings. As she looked she became conscious of a gnarled old man in a cloth cap who had approached in carpet-slippers and now stood beside her.

'Fine tree that,' he had said, following her gaze. 'Been here all my lifetime, it has.'

Anna made a non-committal noise.

'I was born in one of them cottages,' he went on, nodding towards the flint row. 'But 'orrible damp they was, always. I'm round the corner now in a new place. Electric and that. Bit of garden too, but it don't grow flowers all that well.'

Anna remained silent, hoping that he would go away. She had enough depressing thoughts of her own without this garrulous old man, with his unpleasantly moist nose, adding to them. And then he said something which pricked into reality all the numb ache which Anna was enduring.

'Used to be lovely beds of white violets under all our street. Us kids picked 'em in handfuls. I can smell 'em now!'

He sniffed wetly and Anna's distaste was softened by the expression of rapt memory which wrinkled his old red-rimmed eyes.

She wished him good evening and walked on, the words echoing inside her head.

'Lovely beds of white violets under all our street,' she repeated wonderingly to herself, watching her feet tread the hard grey pavements. Beneath them, she thought with a pang, innumerable small beauties of flower, leaf, and convoluting root had smothered and died, remembered only by the very old, ready to die themselves.

It was soon after this that Anna experienced her first Parents' Association meeting.

It had been mentioned casually, in the staff room on the morning of the day in question, by the glamorous Joan Berry. She was sitting on the staff-room table surveying a ladder which was running the length of her elegant leg.

'That leaves one pair for the Parents' do tonight,' she said bitterly. 'Ruination?'

'Do we all have to come?' asked Anna, in some alarm. She had been looking forward to as cosy a domestic evening as Mrs Flynn's bleak premises could offer, intending to wash her hair, write to several friends, and sort out pictures for the walls of her new classroom. This innocent vision seemed about to disappear.

'Hasn't Miss Enderby said anything? She will, don't worry. Our Parent–Teacher Association is one of her hobby-horses.'

'What do we wear?' asked Anna, turning her back bravely upon the domestic evening and facing the new project with a natural womanly reaction.

'Oh, anything,' responded Joan Berry vaguely, hitching up her skirt to study the upper rungs of the ladder which now approached a froth of white underclothes. 'A frock, you know, or a suit. Not slacks, of course – but nothing too dazzling.'

Anna mentally checked over her wardrobe. She was weighing the merits of her tartan frock (loathsomely familiar to her, no shoes to go with it and decidedly spotted about the skirt) against her blue silk suit (too tight across the back, the blouse which looked best with it languishing at home in Essex, and probably much too conspicuous in any case for such an occasion), when the bell put a stop to her speculations.

Miss Enderby spoke of the meeting at prayers and later caught Anna as her class began to swarm up the stairs.

'I should have mentioned it before, dear, but really the beginning of term is so hectic – ' She left the sentence in mid air, and passed a fine hand across her white hair with an air of harassed weariness.

'About half past seven in the hall. All the staff will be here, and the parents are a very friendly set. You'll find meeting them such a help with the children.'

A scuffle at the head of the stairs caused her weariness to vanish in a flash. With remarkable agility for a heavily-built woman she raced up the stairs past the children, who cowered nervously to one side, and plucked a small boy from the landing above.

'To my room!' thundered Miss Enderby in an awe-inspiring boom. She turned flashing eyes upon Anna who had toiled up after her.

'*Jumping*,' said Miss Enderby, outraged, '*jumping*, I say, on his neighbour's toes! The very idea! Perhaps you'd like *me* to jump on yours?'

The child, wide-eyed, surveyed the bulk of his headmistress with acute alarm, and shook his head, too apprehensive to speak.

'We'll see!' Miss Enderby said grimly. She raised a massive arm and pointed towards her door.

Meekly the little boy set off on his lone journey to await judgement, while his classmates, unusually subdued, went into the classroom and the blissful safety of their own desks.

'Be *very* firm, dear, when they are going from one place to another. That's when accidents happen,' said Miss Enderby, in a low aside.

She gave Anna a reassuring smile.

'Don't forget the meeting. You'll enjoy it immensely,' she said, in a voice that brooked no argument, and then set off along the corridor in pursuit of the malefactor.

*

The school hall was ablaze with lights when Anna arrived that evening. She had crept upstairs to leave her coat in the staff room, hoping that the blue silk suit would not look as tight as it felt, and very glad to postpone her entry into the throng which she had glimpsed through the glass of the hall doors.

The cheerful din of crockery being stacked on trays, the clattering of tea spoons, and the exchange of badinage between members of the refreshments committee as they bustled merrily about in the kitchen, receded as Anna climbed towards the merciful silence of the upper floor.

Only 'the moles' were in the cloakroom. These, it had transpired, were two young members of staff, who had been together at the same training college and who now were inseparable, drawn together by past ties and by an incredible likeness in personal appearance and outlook.

They were both small and swarthy, both wore glasses and faint moustaches, and dressed in the same dowdy colours – the curious musty greens and terracotta shades beloved by the Victorians. They were extraordinarily diligent and earnest. As soon as they had bolted down their school dinner they disappeared into their classrooms, there to make gargantuan preparations for the afternoon's hand work, or to concoct strange, up-to-the-minute apparatus for the infants in their charge as shown in the latest number of *Child Education*.

They rarely dallied in the staff room, and looked with some impatience at those who lolled at the table, stirring their after-dinner Nescafé, talking of football pools, clothes, and the current films. In return they were treated with affectionate tolerance by the rest of the staff, who recognized, but did not relish, their dedication to their work.

They were silent creatures and now, as Anna entered, contented themselves with smiling and shifting to let the girl see her reflection in the mirror above the wash-basin. They were busy patting their lank hair into place and dabbing their sallow complexions with tiny discs of powder-puffs about the size of a penny – and much the same colour, as far as Anna could see.

'What happens at these affairs?' she asked nervously. Miss Jones waited for Miss Smith to answer, but, after a full minute, was obliged to give tongue herself.

'People sing, and we dance a bit, and have sandwiches,' she said at last, with a heavy sigh. It certainly sounded the wildest orgy, thought Anna, applying lipstick carefully. She decided not to put too much on. After all, she would like to give the parents of her charges an impression of wholesome gentility, and respectability appeared to be the keynote of the evening. She hoped her skirt was not too short nor her heels too high. It would be dreadful to be thought frivolous. The moles, she noticed, wore their usual flat shoes and their ankles rose from them like sturdy pillars of rectitude.

'Better go down, I suppose,' said Miss Smith resignedly, leading the way. Anna was not sure whether she should accompany the two inseparables, but was so nervous of making her entrance alone that she risked their displeasure by following them closely down the stairs and into the hall.

The school radiogram had been fed with records and was emitting a high-pitched squealing noise which Anna recognized after a few excruciating minutes of concentration as a Scottish reel. Whether the bagpipes or the ancient radiogram's reproduction was to blame for the distressing racket was difficult to decide. About three hundred people, with voices raised above the background cacophony, added to the pandemonium.

Miss Enderby, magnificent in flowered silk, took Anna to meet the chairman of the managers who sat with his wife and a number of friends uncomfortably close to the radiogram. He was incredibly old and frail, his skin stretched like yellow parchment over the fragile bones of his skull. He was very deaf (which Anna could not help feeling was a blessing in his present circumstances) but nodded kindly to Anna and spoke welcomingly to her in an almost inaudible little speech, holding and patting her hand the while.

Dumb show introductions were made and Anna felt quite exhausted with smiling and nodding and mouthing polite nothings under the battery of noise. It was quite a shock when someone switched off the radiogram and only the hubbub of three hundred voices stirred the air.

Miss Enderby mounted the platform and made a brief speech of welcome. She then went on to outline the term's programme and Anna took advantage of the lull to look at the other members of staff who had scattered themselves among the throng. They were all unusually resplendent. Miss Hobbs, her eyes fixed, like some devoted spaniel's watching its master, upon Miss Enderby, wore a man-tailored grey suit and a small diamond brooch. Joan Berry was in a flame-coloured frock, and even the masters appeared comparatively elegant having changed from their usual depressing uniform of baggy grey suits or subfusc hacking jackets.

Her gaze wandered over the assembled parents. They were a

cheerful-looking collection on the whole, she decided, but the sight of so many strange faces filled her with a sudden piercing longing for the small familiar world of her own home. There, at any gathering, she would have known them all. Even in the larger sphere of the market town where she had had her schooling almost all the people were known to her. She had felt that she belonged. But here, in this strange hall, set among the sad ravaged fields, where now no violets grew, she felt overcome with the hopelessness of ever getting to know, or even wanting to know, the host of strangers before her. A sudden vision of the Essex farmhouse appeared in her mind's eye. The lights would be shining out from its comfortable bulk, and from the clump of elms near by the old owl would be slipping down the wind on noiseless wings. A star or two would be studding the night sky. It was almost more than the homesick girl could bear, and it was lucky that at that moment Miss Enderby's little speech ended and Miss Hobbs caught her arm and led her to meet Mrs Crossley who was the mother of a chubby, placid boy in her class.

'He's such a *frail* child,' Mrs Crossley assured her earnestly, 'and terribly sensitive, you know. Just like me, I'm afraid.' She gave a self-conscious laugh and Anna tried to think of a suitable rejoinder.

'He seems very happy at school – ' she began timidly.

'Oh he's wonderfully *plucky*!' asserted Mrs Crossley. From the way she spoke one might have thought that the child was called upon to face torture daily at Anna's hands. She did not add 'Just like me,' to this statement, but her tone implied that the boy's pluckiness as well as his sensitivity was inherited from his mother.

She gave a quick look round, hitched her chair more closely to Anna's and spoke in a lowered voice.

'Of course, I think you should know something about the little chap which I don't usually broadcast.'

Her conspiratorial manner alarmed Anna considerably. She

did so hope that she was not going to hear a number of obstetrical details which so many married ladies seemed to enjoy disclosing.

'Oh please don't – ' began Anna hastily, hoping to spare them both embarrassment. But Mrs Crossley's face wore that disheartening look of one who knows where her duty lies however unpleasant, and Anna braced herself to hear the worst.

'He was a seven-months baby,' whispered Mrs Crossley darkly. Anna nodded and did her best to look suitably impressed.

'No one,' continued Mrs Crossley raising her voice a trifle, '*but no one*, can imagine what I went through with him. It's not surprising that he's still so highly-strung.'

Anna wondered if it would be of any use to tell her that Andrew appeared to be the strongest, noisiest, greediest, and most irrepressible of all her class, but realized that it would simply be waste of breath. The image of an ethereal creature, almost too fragile for this coarse world, was firmly fixed in his mother's mind and it would take more than Anna's testimony to eradicate it.

The arrival of a dish of sausage rolls terminated the conversation and Anna turned thankfully towards Andy Craig who was bearing it round the room. Normally she evaded this particular member of staff. His habit of ruffling his sandy moustache and gazing speculatively at her did not endear him to her, but as a refuge from Mrs Crossley he was more than welcome. He looked surprised and pleased at her unusual warmth of greeting.

'Anything I can get you?' he asked preening himself.

'I ought to meet a few more parents,' said Anna hastily. His face fell, but he gazed round obediently.

'What about old Chapman?' he suggested, pointing to a purple-faced heavy-weight across the room. But old Chapman had to be left for another time, for at that moment the radiogram sprang into hideous life again, someone called 'Take your partners for a quickstep!' and Anna found herself jerking round the room with her face uncomfortably near Andy Craig's R.A.F. tie.

There was really no room to dance. Fathers and mothers, neighbours and friends jogged patiently about together and even the moles were on the floor clamped to the best suits of two perspiring fathers.

'Hell, my wrist!' said Andy Craig, removing a moist palm from Anna's and surveying a yellow leather wrist strap of impressive width.

'What have you done to it?' asked Anna. Andy Craig gave a light laugh.

'Nothing, nothing, my dear. Just a relic of the war days, you know. But there, you wouldn't know – way before your time.' He gave a wince, but bravely replaced his hand.

'Andy Craig, War Hero!' thought Anna mischievously, and then chided herself for being uncharitable. She must find out more about this mysterious war incident, she decided.

The dance over, two of the mothers settled themselves at the piano and gave a spirited, if inaccurate, duet which was warmly applauded. They were followed by an exuberant father who sang "Take a Pair of Sparkling Eyes' ('What again?' had been Andy Craig's audible comment when this was announced), with a sprightly archness which Anna found hard to endure.

She spoke to more parents but felt that she would never remember them if she met them again in one of the muddy half-made streets of this strange new world. As the evening wore on she longed for quietness, for fresh air, and the peace of her country home.

She felt dazed but listened politely to the accounts of her pupils' home life, but the children that their parents spoke of seemed quite different from those same children whom she met in class. Beauty is indeed in the eye of the beholder, thought Anna. She had never before realized how precious, special, and fragile were those in her care, nor how privileged she was to have such riches in her charge.

At the end of the proceedings as she was about to leave the hall, her mind bent on bed and the dubious comforts of Mrs Flynn's establishment, a wispy little woman caught her arm and introduced herself as 'Julia's mummy.'

'Before you go,' she whispered nervously, 'do let me tell you one thing.' Anna smiled reassuringly. Nothing much could be wrong with Julia, she felt sure. She was the bounciest, bonniest extrovert that ever bullied her classmates.

'She may look a big girl,' said her mother, as though divining Anna's thoughts, 'but she's a bundle of nerves really and terribly highly-strung!'

She paused for a moment and looked apprehensively about her at the departing crowd, and Anna had the doomed feeling that this had all happened before.

'It's probably,' she said, dropping her voice to a faint conspiratorial sibilance, 'because she's a seven-months child.'

'Believe me,' Anna heard herself replying earnestly, 'she's not the only one!'

5. A Rum Lot

As the first weeks passed, Anna found her work a little less tiring. No longer did she totter home at four o'clock to her narrow little bed, carefully remove the folk-weave coverlet, and lie exhausted for half an hour before facing Mrs Flynn's dry slab cake and thin tea. Tired she still was at the end of the day, edgy with the constant noise of movement of hundreds of exuberant children, and over-anxious about her ability to keep order and to teach her carefully prepared lessons; but not so completely drained as at first.

Now she was able to take stock of her progress and was amused, and slightly alarmed, to hear herself lapsing into the imbecile speech and turns of phrase which she had so healthily despised in teachers of young children.

'I can see,' she had heard herself say sternly, 'several naughty little people, not a hundred miles from here, who will certainly not be chosen for the Christmas play. I'm looking for two really *trustworthy* rabbits and six sensible *clear-speaking* frogs!'

It wouldn't do at all, she told herself in panic, and yet the dreadful truth was that the children seemed to respond to this way of talking. It was contrary to all the text-books, to Anna's teaching notes taken down so laboriously at college, and to her own dislike of debasing her mother tongue. She decided that she must keep an ear cocked for the treacheries that escaped her lips.

She found herself called upon to teach Scripture, Physical Exercise, Arithmetic, Writing, Reading, English Composition Written and Oral, History, Geography, Nature Study, Art, Handicrafts, Music and Singing, Hygiene, and a mysterious subject called Rhythmic Work which had somehow eluded her during her studies.

'Don't worry,' Miss Enderby had said kindly, when Anna had confessed her ignorance. 'It is all part of our musical training here. Miss Hobbs is particularly competent. You must watch one or two of her lessons.'

And so Anna found herself one afternoon sitting nervously in the corner of the school hall, her notebook open on her lap, watching Miss Hobbs's Rhythmic Work lesson with forty-eight lively nine-year-olds.

'Find a space! Find a space!' Miss Hobbs's hearty voice boomed out as the children struggled through the doors. Little knots of friends charged boisterously about together, intoxicated with the space of the hall after the narrow confines of their desks and the decorous pace demanded by the stone corridors if plain murder were not to result from the passing of masses of children from one part of the building to the other.

Miss Hobbs gave a brusque nod to Anna as she strode towards the piano. A crashing chord caused the majority of the class to stand still. The glare of Miss Hobbs's eye, which swivelled over the top of the piano like a searchlight, stilled the rest within a minute. Anna was overcome with awe at such a demonstration of authority.

'Remember last week's lesson?' boomed Miss Hobbs. 'Butterflies? Off you go.'

Tinkling music in the highest two octaves of the school piano set the children running haphazardly about the hall, flapping their arms. Anna noticed that Miss Hobbs did not seat herself on the piano stool. Most of the class would have been hidden from her sight had she done so. She half-stood, therefore, with her knees bent in a most unbecoming way and kept a sharp look-out for malefactors over the top of the instrument, while her hands led an independent existence of their own scampering vivaciously along the upper keys.

'Up on your toes! On your toes!' exhorted Miss Hobbs above the uproar. 'You sound like a herd of stampeding elephants, Class Four. And don't flail you arms like that, Bobby

Byng. You nearly hit your neighbour just now. You're a *butterfly*, not a mad bull.'

Anna noticed that even Miss Hobbs's discipline was strained by these conditions and felt quite sure that her own frail hold on her class would be snapped asunder as soon as she brought them into the hall, and bedlam would inevitably break out. Several naughty little boys were charging wildly about the hall catching their friends and enemies indiscriminately with blows from their butterfly wings which caused considerable pain and resulted in recrimination. A vicious little set-to was being conducted at the back of the piano, which was out of range of Miss Hobbs's piercing gaze. Only when one of the butterflies stumbled against the piano as the result of a flesh-wound, administered by a fellow-butterfly of powerful physique, did Miss Hobbs realize what was going on. Retribution was swift. Both butterflies were stood one at each side of the hall while the lesson continued.

The children became mettlesome horses, snowflakes, trees in the wind, and waves on the shore. They fell prettily asleep to lullaby music whose soothing whispers were shattered during the slumbrous arpeggios by Miss Hobbs shouting: 'That boy who's snoring can just stop it!' They woke up again to chords so resounding that the windows rattled.

At one stage they sat on the floor bending forward and back rhythmically while Miss Hobbs strode among them intoning: '*Row* the boat, *row* the boat!' and '*Pull* your oars and *pull* your oars!' like an overseer among the galley-slaves. Anna noticed the opportunities this exercise gave for shooting out the legs energetically and kicking one's immediate neighbour.

As she made ineffectual little notes in her book she wondered if she would ever manage to take a Rhythmic Work lesson without having to send for the First Aid box, which was kept, unfortunately, in the room of Miss Enderby herself.

The clock showed that only five minutes more remained of the lesson. The children were beginning to flag but Miss Hobbs, with the physique of an ox and determined to set Anna an inspired example, was as fresh as a daisy. She exhorted them to smell the delicious roses which they held in their hands. Her own weather-beaten face took on an expression of ecstasy as she inhaled the imaginary perfume, but this changed swiftly when forty-eight noses obediently sniffed forty-eight bouquets, and her tone, on demanding the production of handkerchiefs immediately, was peremptory.

As a final exercise the puffing children were told to skip freely about in a beautiful field.

'End the lesson on a note of carefree happiness,' said Miss Hobbs to Anna. It sounded remarkably like a quotation from somebody's Rhythmic Work manual, thought Anna, but she nodded dutifully and prepared to watch.

There was no doubt about it, Miss Hobbs knew her stuff. She had left the piano and now capered from one end of the hall to the other among her stumbling and perspiring companions. She pointed her toes, she bent gracefully to left and right, winning smile set upon her face. As she skipped she chanted rhythmically: 'Skip about, skip about! Smell the flowers. Feel the sun! Hear the birds! A lovely day! Skip for joy! Skip for joy!'

The leaden-footed efforts of the children began to annoy her. Seizing some luckless child by the wrist she bounced it along with her, trying to instil into its lumpish frame some of the energy which drove her own. The rest of the children made a last valiant attempt to emulate their teacher's steps, except for Bobby Byng, a slow adenoidal child who had a mulishness which was at its worst in Rhythmic Work.

Out of the corner of her eyes, Miss Hobbs, still capering in the sprightliest manner, caught sight of the boy. He was standing absolutely still! It was too much. Dropping her bouncing partner, she flew to Bobby Byng's side and administered a resounding slap on the boy's leg.

'*Now* will you skip for joy?' she boomed wrathfully.

Anna averted her gaze hastily from Miss Hobbs's scarlet face and looked at her notebook.

'End the lesson,' it said blandly, 'on a note of carefree happiness.'

On many occasions Anna had cause to remember Joan Berry's remark about the staff being 'a rum lot – a very rum lot'.

Joan Berry herself was unique on the staff for her elegance of appearance and for her thinly disguised contempt and amusement at her colleagues' coiffures and costumes. From her spike-heeled shoes to the top of her outrageous hats she was a vision of delight to unsophisticated Anna, used as she was to country clothes of a more utilitarian design. Clothes were Joan Berry's overriding passion and with their help she expressed not only her flair for line and colour but also her disdain of those who lacked such interest. Anna was secretly appalled at the amount of money which she spent on her appearance. She had seen Joan Berry's dressing table with its rows and ranks of bottles and jars lined up like soldiers in battle array ready to keep the enemies, wrinkles, flabbiness, spots, and blemishes, at a distance. She compared it with her own modest lipstick, cold cream, and powder, and stood amazed. To spend so much time, thought, and money upon such things seemed out of all proportion to Anna.

It wasn't as though it made Joan any happier, Anna thought. The older girl's passionate interest drove her to gaze in shop windows at shoes and furs and jewels which it gave her real pain to eschew. It was as if some insatiable secret hunger could be alleviated by a stream of new adornments, of one sort or another, yet never really satisfied. It puzzled Anna very much.

The redoubtable Miss Hobbs's outstanding passion was for her headmistress which expressed itself in a fierce loyalty which Anna found embarrassing at times. When Miss Enderby expressed a wish to see Anna's record book in which she kept her notes for her week's work, it was maddening to have Miss Hobbs say brusquely: 'And mind it's handed in at once! Miss Enderby's overworked as it is, and doesn't want to have to run around after you!' Such devotion may have had its admirable side once, but taken to such irritating excess it simply made Miss Hobbs appear ridiculous in the sight of her younger and more ribald colleagues.

Miss Smith and Miss Jones, the two moles, were set apart by their earnest overwork. As far as Anna could judge they spent their evening solely in the continuance of school work, making apparatus, filling in records, filing pictures, and the like. She had never heard them mention a theatre, a cinema, a television programme, or any book not immediately connected with education. They were a daunting pair, but Anna found them pitiful too.

Andy Craig, of the gooseberry eyes and damaged wrist, she felt no pity for. He was lazy, vain, and boastful, and his jejune attempts at lady-killing irritated Anna. Occasionally the wide wrist-strap was exchanged for a sling made from a spotted silk scarf.

'What's the matter with Mr Craig's wrist?' asked Anna innocently of Joan Berry one day.

'Don't give him the satisfaction of asking,' said Joan shortly.

'But is it serious? I heard him say something about the war. Was he shot down?'

'That's what he'd like you to think,' said Joan grimly. 'But the nearest he ever got to an aeroplane was pulling the chocks away. As a matter of fact he got his arm caught in a swing door at his R.A.F. camp. I happen to know someone who was there with him – but dear Andy doesn't know that. I must say I get a lot of secret fun out of his antics. Still it's an innocent conceit, I suppose, and hurts no one. The old inferiority complex, my child. Put it down to the usual bogy!'

They certainly were a rum lot, Anna thought, and the more you got to know them the rummer they became. She had taken a liking to middle-aged Mr Foster because he seemed so pleasantly normal, a shabbier and more vague edition of her uncles. He had two children, much about her own age, she knew, and a wife who taught part-time to help make ends meet. She first became aware of Mr Foster's secret ambition when she had a free period one wet morning and they were alone in the staff room.

Anna was busy at one end of the table, correcting a pile of English exercises. At the other end Mr Foster scribbled industriously in an exercise book. Occasionally he sighed through the mists of blue cigarette smoke that wreathed around him. At last he set down his ball-point pen with a clatter, blew wetly at the cigarette ash which he had dribbled down his crumpled jacket, and spoke to his companion.

'Ever do any writing?' he asked.

'Only letters,' answered Anna, startled from her marking. It was obvious that Mr Foster was disposed to talk, and Anna put down her own marking pencil. 'Why? Do you?' she asked.

Mr Foster waved a pudgy hand deprecatingly at the exercise book before him.

'Oh, I'm always at it. Had a go at pretty well everything in the writing line.'

'Have you had anything published?' asked Anna with proper awe. She was glad to see that Mr Foster looked gratified and guessed, rightly, that he had.

'One or two little things,' he admitted with a very fair show of *insouciance*. He tapped his cigarette ash carefully into the empty carton he had put on the table, and watched his own operations through narrowed, world-weary eyelids.

'How lovely!' said Anna enthusiastically. 'What in?'

A shade of annoyance seemed to quirk Mr Foster's puffy countenance, but he answered readily enough.

'Well, I had a review on a woodwork manual in a teachers' paper last year, and a country magazine accepted a poem of mine some months ago.'

'A poem!' breathed Anna admiringly.

'Of course you don't get a lot of money from Poetry,' Mr Foster hastened to explain, with the air of one who tosses off half-a-dozen odes before shaving, 'but it's good training in the *Use of Words*.'

'Naturally,' agreed Anna.

'Where the *money* is,' went on Mr Foster, warming to his theme, 'is in books for the twelves to fifteens. That's what this is.' He held up the exercise book. 'It's really a novel for young people. The publishers are falling over themselves for downright, realistic stories, with a working-class background, for teenagers. Aimed at the secondary moderns, you know – and showing the home background. This chap – my hero – has a drunken father and a mother out at work. He has to dress the younger children and give them breakfast before going off to school himself. Of course he's appeared in the juvenile court once or twice, and in the next chapter I'm having a pretty strong scene with the Probation Officer. Oh, I think it will be acceptable to schools and libraries too.'

'But surely,' protested Anna, 'that's not a true picture of an average secondary modern schoolboy? Why, lots of my friends at home went to our local school till they were fifteen, and I can't think of one of them who had a drunken father – except perhaps on Harvest Home night or Christmas Eve,' she added, as an honest afterthought.

'The country, my dear,' said Mr Foster, heavily avuncular, 'is a very different kettle of fish from our large towns!'

'But even so – all this talk of juvenile courts and Probation Officers –' expostulated Anna.

'Life in the raw!' Mr Foster assured her pontifically. He rummaged in a baggy pocket, produced a catapult, two pieces of chalk, and a grubby handkerchief before discovering the packet of cigarettes for which he was searching. Anna watched his fumblings indignantly, like a small ruffled owl. It was true she knew mighty little of life in large towns but she was positive that Mr Foster's picture was grossly overdrawn.

'The other thing that brings the money in,' went on Mr Foster, blissfully unaware of Anna's inward smoulderings, 'is a thoroughly good text-book. Say, a series in English. Four books, one for each year of the primary school. Why, some of those chaps who got in early must have made a fortune!'

His moist eyes brightened at the thought.

'Think of the numbers one school alone would have to order! Forty-eight in a class, say. That's four dozen for each year. Sixteen dozen!'

Mr Foster's normally flat tones grew quite sharp with enthusiasm. He turned his exercise book sideways and began to do excited little sums in the rather wide margins.

'Sixteen dozen a school – let's say five hundred schools –' he began busily, pencil flying. His voice dropped to incoherent whisperings as he worked out his multiplication sums.

Anna's indignation subsided as she watched him. There he sat, a great flabby, hulk of a man, living in the dream-world of Get-Rich-Quick. She thought suddenly of her father and the work that went into one of his fields of wheat which he would be harvesting now. He too would be thinking of the rewards of his labours, but he would have done the major part of them before counting his gains. To see the man before her exciting himself, like a greedy child, at the thought of vast wealth for something which had not even been started and which, Anna suspected, never would be started, let alone completed, filled her with disgust tempered with pity.

Joan Berry was right, mused Anna. They certainly are a rum lot! She cast her mind over the other two male members of staff, of whom she had seen little. One of them, John Fraser, was newly married and lived in a particularly horrible house near the school, with windows containing panes of coloured glass in the form of tulips. He was the last member of staff to enter the school gates and the first to leave at night. Only his newly-married state had kept him so far from Miss Enderby's verbal disapproval. The rest of the staff, left to cope with his unruly class in the cloakrooms, sincerely hoped that retribution would come upon him before long. There must be an end some time to Miss Enderby's romantic tolerance.

The fourth and last male member was Tom Drew, a dark young man, entering upon his second year of teaching and saying very little to anyone. Anna had exchanged only half-a-dozen sentences with him since she arrived, but she liked him and guessed that he missed the countryside home from which he had come as much as she did her own.

It was he who came into the staff room just as Mr Foster looked up, flushed and happy, from his sums.

'At ten per cent, I make it almost a thousand pounds!' he said exuberantly.

'It'd be guineas in the literary world,' said Tom Drew, lighting a cigarette.

'So it would! So it would!' agreed Mr Foster, returning to his calculations with even greater fervour.

Tom's eyes met Anna's in a dark amused glance and Anna felt curiously happy. Could this possibly be an exception among such a very rum lot?

6. Genuine Articles

HOME at the weekends became doubly dear. The journey from Elm Hill across the sprawling mass of London seemed interminable, but once clear of the eastern suburbs Anna's heart rose higher with every mile that passed.

As summer changed to autumn the trees near her home deepened in colour from fading green to gold and then to bronze, and Anna looked out for these much-loved landmarks weekly and noted the change that each week wrought in them.

The joy of home-coming was ever fresh. The smell of the old farmhouse compounded of years of wood smoke, stone floors, and the linseed oil which was used to polish the ancient oak staircase, was like a benison to Anna, after the bleak gas-tainted air which greeted her as Mrs Flynn's front door yielded grudgingly to her pressure. The feel of the old flagstones in the farmhouse hall, worn and uneven from generations of sturdy boots, gave Anna a lift of the heart which Mrs Flynn's impersonal, even linoleum could never do: and the sight of the great fireplace, a cavern of glowing wood from her father's fields, flinging a wide welcome of cheerful warmth, made Anna realize how thoroughly she loathed Mrs Flynn's meagre gas fire, with row upon row of little white skulls looking like some tidy, ghastly, miniature Golgotha.

Anna had time to ponder over the differences one autumn evening when her parents had gone to visit a neighbouring farmer. The fire crackled and leaped. Little red-hot twigs snapped and fell into the glowing ash, sending up spurts of yellow flame which were reflected in the pieces of copper and the old polished furniture in the darkening room. It was a joyous living thing with movement, noise, and colour of its own. Mrs Flynn's carefully adjusted gas fire gave only a hint of its presence with its faint warmth and sibilant hissing. It was no gay company as the farmhouse fire was, thought Anna, watching the latter lazily through half-closed eyes.

It was the same with the food. At Mrs Flynn's Anna never saw an identifiable joint of meat. She supposed that such a thing might conceivably find its way into Mrs Flynn's kitchen at the weekend when she was not there. Certainly rissoles, cottage pies, and other meat concoctions appeared occasionally for supper and these might have been the residue of an earlier joint. But here, at home, Anna saw a leg of mutton or a loin of pork brought sizzling and savoury from the oven, and her appetite was whetted at once. The apples that she peeled were great golden beauties from the tree in the garden. She had lain in the shade in the hot July sunshine and looked up at them when they had been hard green pom-poms among the young leaves. But Mrs Flynn's apples were bruised from much travelling and their smell was as much of the blue tissue paper in which they had been wrapped for so long as of the fragrant apple itself.

Anna thought of the celery she had prepared for tea. It had been freshly dug that afternoon and was thick with moist black soil which she had watched swirl away in the sink under the onslaught of the tap water. The celery was left glistening and pearly. She had cut through its cold, crisp heart and a slim young worm, pink and agile, had made his escape when she parted the stalks. The celery which Anna had seen stacked in the Elm Hill shops had looked dull and flabby, patched with rusty brown. It would have made a poor home for any self-respecting worm, she thought.

She recalled too the conversation she had overheard between two old countrymen who had boarded the Green Line coach that evening on its last stage. Their voices were warm and burred and they talked slowly of everyday country matters. One had had a fine crop of runner beans. His wife had salted some down. Tomorrow he was going to shift his pig into that little copse at the end of his garden. The other said that last week's rain had 'come down a treat – been a real blessing, it had', and Anna thought wryly of the comments of the Elm Hill people on that same day's rain as they had queued miserably for buses or complained of splashed stockings. In the country the rain's blessing could be seen. Trees, flowers, and plants reached up refreshed and the birds splashed in puddles and noisily relished newly-found worms. In the town the rain was simply a nuisance, drumming on the hard pavements and forming pools for unwary and flimsily-shod feet to encounter, and dripping from shop blinds on to expensive hats. And to Mrs Flynn and her like, rain meant only one thing – an unneccessary mess trodden in.

One phrase in the old men's conversation stuck in Anna's mind. They had been talking of a neighbour's well, how deep it was, and how cold the water even on the hottest day.

'Ah!' said one meditatively and with deep appreciation, 'that's lovely – water is – straight from the spring!'

It was a simple statement of fact, but to Anna, repeating it to herself, it sounded like poetry, for she had her mother's ear for such things. It gave her great comfort to think that such a lovely phrase had come from the appreciation of something so elemental and so everyday. Where in Elm Hill, she wondered, would she meet anyone who praised, so splendidly, the water that flowed from his gleaming taps?

The next day she and her mother walked to the village to buy a loaf. They crossed one of their own fields, to take a short cut, and were watched by a herd of curious young bullocks who watched their passing with large, liquid, unblinking eyes. Anna wondered what went on beneath those curly polls – hope of food, apprehension, or simply a vague interest in another moving animal?

The hedges were full of colour and the two picked sprays of

bright yellow hornbeam and rose hips to decorate the house. The autumn air was delicious to Anna, with a tang about it that reminded her of nuts and rustling leaves underfoot and other joys of the dying year.

She chattered animatedly to her mother about life at Elm Hill and tried to put into words not only the difference in outlook between the people she had met there and those in the village, which she had pondered the night before, but more particularly the foibles of the members of Elm Hill school's staff.

'They all seem to have something odd about them,' explained Anna, frowning with concentration. 'There's Andy Craig, being mysterious about a war wound and hoping we'll think him a hero. Then there's Joan Berry – whom I like, mind you,' she added hastily, 'but she's always in an absolute fever about clothes or her hair or some infinitesimal spot no one can see. And even Miss Enderby sighs over a sapphire ring as though she hopes you'll ask her about the Great Tragedy in her life!'

'They're no odder than the people here,' responded her

mother. 'Look at Miss Chubb and Miss Bower and that wretched hedge of theirs they're always squabbling about.' The two maiden ladies in question kept up a pleasurable feud over the boundary of their adjoining gardens, and the rest of the village had to be on guard when meeting one or the other in case more fuel were added to the fire by a misplaced word either of sympathy or censure. Mrs Lacey had not lived in a village without meeting the dangers that spring from an unguarded tongue.

They reached the stile that bordered the lane leading to the village and the baker's. Mrs Lacey stood thoughtfully athwart it, one foot firmly planted on each side of the crossbar, and gazed reflectively into the distance. Anna looked up at her parent with merriment. There she stood, engrossed in her thoughts, clutching to her the wild lovely bouquet which would later give her so much pleasure in the farmhouse, so different, Anna commented again, from the faded artificial daffodils which Mrs Flynn dusted carefully each day. Ah, *that* was it! thought Anna triumphantly. *That* was the simple difference between her two abodes. One was genuine, wholesome and homely – the real thing. The other was false and artificial. The words of a pretty and plaintive song that she had heard her mother sing, flashed into her mind:

> It's a Barnum and Bailey world,
> Just as phoney as it can be,

and she was about to share that moment of truth with her mother, but found that she was still mentally pursuing the oddities of her neighbours, on her high perch.

'Take the Charltons and that quite dreadful boy of theirs they're so horribly proud of. They talk of nothing else but the dreary examinations he's passed.' Mrs Lacey stepped briskly off the stile and into the lane.

'Or poor old Captain Lett,' went on Mrs Lacey, warming to her theme, 'with those interminable stories about life in the

North West Passage, or Frontier, or wherever-it-was, in 1905. They drive us all mad, but they do him good, poor old dear.'

She stopped suddenly in the road and gazed at her daughter with intensity.

'That's it, of course,' she cried. 'They're odd – both your people and mine – because they are clinging to something to make them look more important than they really are. It makes them different, and more impressive, they hope, than the rest of us.'

'Well, I think it makes them look pathetic,' answered her daughter sturdily, one hand on the knob of the shop door.

'I don't agree,' said her mother slowly. 'I think it makes them more lovable.'

The village grocer was a large cheerful man who had known Anna all her life and took a great interest in her new job. He was also the village baker, and he led the way to the bakehouse at the rear of the shop across a narrow paved yard.

Anna had always loved the bakehouse. It smelt deliciously of Mr Crook's far-famed doughnuts and lardy cakes and was a warm fragrant haven on a cold winter's day. An enormous scrubbed wooden table stood in the centre and wooden racks near by held the crusty loaves as they aired.

Anna thought of Mrs Flynn's flabby wrapped slices of bread as she surveyed the beauties lined up before her. There were fat cottage loaves with a generous dimple in their crusty tops, long golden 'twists', oval-topped wholemeals, Coburgs with four perky ears, and double-length quarterns which would be taken, Anna knew, to a boarding school or two near by. A batch of small rolls on a separate wire tray meant that someone in the village was giving a party. Mr Crook made those specially, for there was no particular demand for such refinements every day in the village.

Propped against the whitewashed wall near the great oven were two long wooden shovels or peels, which were used to lift the hot loaves out; and in the corner an enormous mixer already held the flour and other dry ingredients ready for the next batch of loaves. On the red brick floor clean flour sacks were spread, and Mr Crook's smoke-grey cat lolled upon one of them, washing a paw indolently and enjoying the luxurious warmth around her.

It did one's heart good, thought Anna, remembering the flash of truth which had illumined the clouds in her mind during the walk, to see something so genuine. She looked with new affection at Mr Crook as he busily shrouded her mother's lovely loaf in generous swathes of tissue paper. He looked as cleanly comfortable and as warmly cheering as his own bake-house, and with his lifelong knowledge of the community which he served he had his place as surely in village affairs as the parson, the schoolmaster, and the doctor.

And where else, thought Anna, as they made their farewells at the shop door, would you find a man willing to spend his Christmas morning cooking innumerable turkeys because his neighbours' ovens were too small, as she knew Mr Crook would be doing before long?

'Not in Elm Hill, I'll be bound!' said Anna aloud, and then laughed at her mother's astonished face.

PART TWO

Finding Roots

7. Occupational Hazards

ANNA's affection for her class grew as the weeks passed. The children were at the stage she liked best – old enough to be able to work and read on their own and yet young enough to be unselfconscious and keen to learn. Their zest for every kind of activity was incredible, and Anna found that provided she could supply a variety of educational tasks for them to do, all was well; but should they ever come to the end of a piece of work and have to wait for attention, then trouble began. The old adage about Satan finding mischief for idle hands to do was certainly in line with the teaching of Anna's tutors and her own growing experience.

The one great, glaring, wicked problem to Anna was the size of her class. Fond of them as she was as individuals, collectively they constituted an unwieldy, noisy, and exhausting mass. The physical difficulty alone of taking a long, long line of forty-eight children about the corridors was tremendous, and Anna suffered much anxiety as she saw energetic leaders vanishing round one corner on the ground floor while the rest still straggled down dangerous stone stairs and along their own corridor above. It was impossible to watch them all, and one high-spirited push would do much damage. One small boy was lame, with his leg in irons, and though Anna let him follow last in the line and put him in the especial care of a sensible friend, he was an added hazard to all their many expeditions.

In the daily physical training sessions in the vast playground Anna found that her voice was often unheard – sometimes, she knew, wilfully – but quite often because the noise of passing traffic, aeroplanes, or the wind that swept the flat wastes, blew the sound away. The freedom of space and air went to the children's heads like wine and Anna always returned to the classroom with mixed feelings. She hated to leave the open air, but was relieved to get her charges back into conditions in which she could manage them more easily.

The classroom, of course, was far too full. Desks were crammed together and such close quarters meant jogged elbows (both by accident and design), kicked legs, and the general irritation engendered by neighbours breathing on each others' necks, overlooking each other's work, and playing with each other's property. To Anna, who had been trained to allow freedom of movement and a certain amount of talking in the classroom, the conditions were doubly frustrating. She found herself bound to quell quite legitimate noise for the simple reason that she was trying to deal with twice its normal volume, and the free traffic of children from their desks to the shelves and cupboards to fetch their own working materials had to be severely restricted. Monitors were chosen to give out the apparatus required, and Anna was amused to notice that, quite unconsciously, she seemed to have appointed the four smallest children for this task, those that could thread their way more nimbly in the meagre space left between the classroom furniture.

It perturbed her too to think how little time she could conscientiously give to each child. She liked to mark all written work with the child beside her, but soon found that this was impossible to do every time with over forty children. She set herself to hear each child read at least twice a week, and knew in her heart that it should be a daily exercise if conditions would allow. When an epidemic of influenza swept the school, towards the end of her first term, Anna was astonished to find how light and rewarding it was to teach thirty children and how much less strained the atmosphere of her classroom. More than once she thought of the village school at home where about fifty children were divided between three teachers. Despite the difference in the range of age, and the difficulties this raised, Anna envied those three heartily. No wonder they looked cheerful and motherly and had time and energy to chat in the lane as they wheeled their bicycles beside the mothers, thought Anna.

The question of the placing of desks had presented some problems to Anna who had been told that 'never, never, should they be in straight rows facing the blackboard', by an earnest lecturer at college.

'As informal as possible,' she had emphasized. 'Let friends put their desks together and get to know how to work with each other. Turn the desks this way and that as the lesson demands. Make a lovely big work-table for cutting-out activities by pushing four or six together. Or make a cosy half-circle ready for story time and the picture-drawing session after it. Be imaginative with your space and your furniture!' she had exhorted her pupils.

Anna often thought of this good advice as she wryly surveyed her jammed classroom. There never seemed to be time, let alone space, to plan all these manoeuvres, and the sound of forty-six desks, forty-six chairs, and their forty-six owners would have been almost too much, even for Anna's healthy young nerves.

She had, after many experiments, evolved a system which seemed to combine a certain informality with ease of movement and yet allowed each child to see the blackboard which ran across the width of the wall behind her desk. She was rather proud of her arrangements, but criticism was soon to come – not from Miss Enderby, who approved the final pattern – but from a visiting inspector.

Anna was amazed at the consternation with which his advent was greeted by the staff of Elm Hill. She had always imagined that an inspector's primary purpose was to help and advise teachers. She had certainly known no reason why she should fear them, so that the trepidation felt by the older members of the staff, in the face of these necessary visitors, surprised her.

It was probably a legacy from the bad old days of 'payment-by-results' of which she had heard.

The first she knew of Mr Andrews's approach was the dramatic entry of Miss Hobbs into her classroom.

'He's come!' she announced, eyes flashing.

For one dreadful moment Anna thought she must be referring to a dangerous lunatic who had escaped two days before from the local hospital and still remained at large. She was weighing up the merits of sending her class home immediately against those of barricading the door and submitting to a state of siege until the local fire brigade could be summoned to evacuate the children from the windows, when Miss Hobbs elucidated a few further details.

'An inspector, Mr Andrews. A fiend incarnate, dear. And has a phobia about lighting. He's with Miss Enderby now. Thought I'd warn you.'

'But what is there to do about it?' inquired Anna, bewildered but reasonable.

'Well, you might see your cupboards are tidy,' suggested Miss Hobbs, already retreating to fly to the next classroom with the dire tidings. 'He's the one that opens cupboard doors.'

'Then he'll have the lot falling out on him in here,' retorted Anna to Miss Hobbs's receding back. The skinny red-haired door monitor, who rejoiced in the name of Gabrielle Pugg, had barely time to close the door behind her before it opened again and Miss Enderby entered with Mr Andrews in tow.

Introductions were made and the children rose politely, if tardily, after a few menacing grimaces from their head teacher. Gabrielle attended to her duties and Miss Enderby left Mr Andrews in Anna's care.

He was a portly little man, with a pink, gleaming, bald head and bright blue eyes which Anna saw were fixed anxiously on the windows which ran down the side of the room. He looked, with growing agitation, at the row of children who sat with their backs to the window as a result of Anna's careful arrangement of the desks.

'Oh dear, dear, dear!' clucked Mr Andrews, hastening across the room. 'This will never do! Never do at all! We must alter this, my dear young lady, before their eyesight is quite ruined!'

Anna thought that he was uncommonly like the White Rabbit in his fussy anxiety.

'Jump up, children, jump up!' he exhorted the long row of delighted boys and girls, waving his plump hands up and down energetically. In various parts of the classroom other children leapt joyously to their feet, only too glad of an excuse. The noise almost drowned Mr Andrews's running commentary, delivered rather breathlessly as he began to drag the desks into a line, one behind the other, facing the blackboard.

'Can't have them sitting in their own light,' puffed Mr Andrews, stepping heavily on to a child's foot. 'I can't think why you haven't been told of it before –'

'It's difficult to fit the numbers in,' began Anna. 'It seemed the best way –'

'Never mind the numbers,' said Mr Andrews grandly, as though a dozen or so excess children could easily be disposed of in the waste-paper basket. 'The first essential of any classroom is Correct Lighting!'

He paused for a minute in his labours, partly to regain his breath and partly to wag an admonitory finger at Anna. The hubbub, she noticed with alarm, was becoming tremendous as the children threw themselves into desk-shoving with joyful and aimless abandon.

'The light must *at all times*, and at *whatever cost*, come from the left-hand side. In that way the child works with the light on his paper, unshaded by his body or his working right hand.'

'What about the left-handed ones?' asked Anna, beginning to feel rebellious at the wagging finger.

Mr Andrews looked a trifle taken aback but recovered with commendable aplomb.

'They must be catered for separately,' he said firmly, bending to his task again. Anna wondered if this meant that one or two classrooms should be reversed in the architects' plans and labelled 'For Left-Handers Only'. There was no end to the complications if one really let oneself go.

The noise was now so great that Anna felt that the best thing was to settle Mr Andrews's desks as he wanted before trying to quieten her class again. In any case, he seemed oblivious to the chaos around him, tugging busily at the furniture and brushing aside any children who crossed his path. After ten minutes' furious work he had all the desks facing front in the style most deplored by Anna's college tutor. She waited, in secret amusement, for the next move.

'Now, children,' said Mr Andrews, wiping a glistening forehead with a neat white square of folded handkerchief. 'Put your chairs behind your desks and let us see how you look.'

As Anna knew, this simple request proved impossible to obey. About half the children – the quicker half – squeezed themselves into place by dint of shifting their desks forward a little. The slower twenty-odd did their valiant best to manhandle their chairs, with vigour and appalling noise, into the minute space available. Anger made their complaints more than usually vociferous, and the smug gaze of those already seated did nothing to alleviate the grievance of those unseated.

'No room miss!'

'They've pinched my place, miss!'

'We're all squashed up, miss. Can't get in here nowhere!'

So rang the despairing cries, and Anna began to feel quite sorry for Mr Andrews and wondered how he would cope with the situation. She need not have wasted her sympathy.

Mr Andrews, who must have faced this dilemma many times, appeared impervious to the complaints and turned a happy face to Anna.

'That's the way to have the desks, my dear. The only way! Don't let anyone try to get you to alter them. Light over the left shoulder, remember!'

He nodded cheerfully and made his way to the door. Gabrielle was not quick enough to keep pace with his brisk trot.

'I'll try and call in again before I leave,' he said to the flabbergasted Anna, left among the chaos of her class, and then vanished through the door.

Anna soon found that Mr Andrews was not unique in being a monomaniac. Visitors to her classroom were frequent. Some were inspectors, some were salaried advisers on a particular subject, some students on educational visits, and others were friends of the school.

The inspectors and advisers Anna had expected, for her first year of teaching was probationary and she knew that she would be under surveillance but she had not expected so much vigilance.

There was another reason for the spate of callers, she discovered. Elm Hill was only a small part of the great new suburb which sprawled further and further across the fields to the north-west of London. The education authority was hard-pressed to keep pace with the rapid growth of population. New schools, new teachers, and new methods abounded, and the inspectorate was kept busy as well as the builders.

Many young teachers like Anna had been appointed straight from college to keep pace with the growing mass of pupils and these needed particular supervision. When, as in Anna's case, the building was grossly overcrowded and a new school due to open near by, even more interested officials from head-quarters came to pay visits, and Anna came to view these callers with dismay.

The advisers, she thought, were the most trying. Each, rather naturally, felt that his own particular subject was the

most important on the time-table and gave so many suggestions, not only for classroom work but for out-of-school
activities and involved apparatus to be constructed by Anna,
that the poor girl felt quite overwhelmed. These zealous souls,
each riding his own hobby-horse, did not seem to see that
Anna faced daily two fearsome foes – too many children and
not enough time. True, they were sympathetic, in a perfunc-
tory way, about the difficulties which confronted her; but
Anna suspected that overcrowded conditions and pressure of
time were such commonplaces to them, and their own burning
passion consumed them so remorselessly, that they lost all
sense of proportion and, as specialists, expected from the hard
pressed teachers they hoped to inspire far more than those
bewildered general practitioners could possibly give, no
matter how willing they might be.

Anna felt at her most helpless when the adviser for arithmetic had had her in her clutches. She had arrived on a morning of torrential rain and wind. One of the classroom windows
had defied all efforts to close it, and the roaring wind played
havoc with the papers on the children's desks. Rain had spattered in and Anna, much-tried and irritable, had moved some
of the desks to the further side of the classroom.

Outside, the cement-mixer rattled merrily and the thudding
of another machine told of the birth of the new infants' building, scheduled to be opened next September, in the same field
as the present school.

The children were restless and worked uninterestedly at
their sum books. The lowest group were having some
difficulty in multiplying by five despite Anna's efforts,
when the door opened and Miss Birch introduced herself.
She looked, more in sorrow than in anger, upon the little
band of children plying their pens and struggling with their
fives.

'You've done plenty of *active* work about *five*, of course?'
she queried.

'Of course,' echoed Anna. 'And in any case, the infant department copes with –'

'The infant department may do,' interrupted Miss Birch forcefully, 'but I hope you continue that good work.'

Anna began, with sinking heart, to submit herself to yet another homily.

'Are they ready to work in the abstract?' pursued Miss Birch. 'Do they *know* five? Do they *experience* five? Have they got a *real feeling* of *fiveness*?'

'I think so,' Anna faltered, 'and in any case they know they've got five fingers on each hand,' she added more bravely.

'Ah!' pounced Miss Birch. 'They may have – but in a row! Now, I do feel most strongly that they should see five in a *pattern*, in a *cluster*, in a *five-group*, which is automatically flashed into their mind's eye when they hear the number five!' She warmed to her theme and Anna's battered senses began to wander.

At the back of the room Arnold had his pen poised close to the cheek of his unsuspecting neighbour. Within a minute, Anna knew from bitter experience, he would call his friend and thus impale his victim's cheek on his nib. It was a simple trick which gave the innocent child much pleasure, and there were still a number of gullible classmates who had not yet had the wit to avoid the trap. Two more boys were having a tongue-stretching match, their eyes hideously crossed.

Children whispered, sniggered, fidgeted, copied each other's work, snatched each other's books, and tormented each other's persons in a dozen irritating ways, while Miss Birch's voice rolled remorselessly on. At last, Anna could bear it no longer.

'Excuse me,' she said, firmly, and advancing to the front desks gave a fair imitation of Miss Enderby's ear-splitting clapping. Hush fell.

'Get on with your work without a word!' said Anna sharply. 'There will be no play for those who talk!'

Meekly, with a martyred air, the children returned to their

labours. Miss Birch watched with a reproving eye such heavily repressive methods. Anna could see that she was debating whether she should make some comment on these harsh dicta, so very much in contradiction to her own free activity, but evidently she decided against it, preferring, Anna had no doubt, to make a dignified note, couched in psychological terms, in the report which she would make later on this visit.

With the air of one wishing to change a painful subject for one of agreeable interest Miss Birch opened a leather case and emptied a large number of rings of assorted colour and size upon Anna's table.

'While they're busy,' she said, her eyes lighting up with enthusiasm, 'I'll explain this simply wonderful method of teaching mathematics. Have you met it?'

Anna confessed that she had not, and secretly viewed the project with the greatest misgiving. There was hardly enough room for a book and a pen on each desk, let alone a mountain of assorted rings, and the thought of the numbers that would fall by accident, be projected by design, and generally find their way floorwise accompanied by their own and their owner's noise, appalled her, but she did her best to look happily responsive as Miss Birch handled the rings affectionately and positively crooned to herself over them.

'You can *actually prove*,' said Miss Birch, looking at poor Anna with a fanatic light in her bright blue eyes, 'H.C.F. and L.C.M.!'

'Really!' said Anna faintly, watching Miss Birch's nimble hands pounce here and there. In a trice she had taken a handful of rings and arranged them into a pattern.

'I'll show you,' said Miss Birch inexorably. And for the next ten minutes, to her uncomprehending but quiescent pupil, she did.

Later that day in the staff room, Anna was relieved to find that she was not the only one so bedevilled.

Miss Hobbs, bridling with outraged self-esteem, had met her match in a smooth-faced young man, known as the newly-appointed county musical adviser, who had watched one of Miss Hobbs's celebrated rhythmic lessons and had criticized it mercilessly.

'He said it was "*too martial*", if you ever heard such rot!' fumed Miss Hobbs, puffing explosively at a cigarette, 'and that they should *never* march in, or be directed to do things that I say. And the music he suggested!'

Miss Hobbs flung her eyes heavenwards.

' "Woodland Frolics" and "Sousa's Marches" which have been my standby for years have been just tossed aside! Look at this list!' She unrolled a paper on which several titles were written in a flowery italic hand in green ink.

'Prokoviev, Shostakovitch, Bartok – the lot!' said Miss Hobbs, dramatically, 'and not one in less than six flats, I'll be bound! If it weren't for backing up dear Florence I'd have told that young man what I thought of him!'

8. An Everyday Young Man

CHRISTMAS approached, and Anna began to count the days to her return home. The thought of the quiet countryside, with its bare sleeping trees and empty brown fields, was like a benison amidst the mounting excitement of the exuberant children and the fraying tempers of her fellow teachers.

The draggle-tail shops of Elm Hill began to deck themselves in tawdry finery. Fly-blown paper bells and balls hung in newsagents' windows, and blobs of cotton-wool, strung on thread, simulated snow in the little greengrocer's shop which Anna passed each morning. The piles of flaccid cabbages and sprouts were enlivened by boxes of dates and a silver-papered tangerine or two which appeared among them like some strange exotic blooms in a winter field.

Even Mrs Flynn had caught the infection and had made Christmas puddings from an 'Economical Wartime Recipe' which satisfied her frugal soul and involved a prodigious proportion of shredded carrots. She had been buying, for some time, only the soap powder which offered free Christmas wrapping papers: 'For,' as she remarked to Anna, 'it's just silly to spend money on something that will be thrown away; and yet one doesn't like to look mean.'

Mrs Flynn's economies, Anna realized after several weeks' experience, were the offspring of two strong urges. The first was her inborn love of a bargain and a burning ambition to make sixpence do where another woman would use a shilling, and the second and stronger urge was to appear a little more comfortably-off and genteel than her neighbours. Anna could forgive the first, but not the second, of these reasons for her landlady's cheese-paring efforts. She had not met, in the country world she knew best, quite such petty ambition. Perhaps it was because people's affairs were more generally known, perhaps her own family minded less than most about outward show – Anna could not tell; but this vying with one's neighbours was a new thing to her. Absorbed interest in others' affairs she recognized only too well, as do all country dwellers, and the diverse pattern of lives influenced by thrift, industry, shiftlessness, and illness was as fascinating to her as her own life was to her neighbours; but it was an interest born of true neighbourliness and not a shallow and spiteful assessment of others for the purpose of self-glorification.

Anna had been shocked one day by Mrs Flynn's bitter contempt for the family next door. They had moved in soon after term began and Mrs Flynn's inspection from behind the top floor curtains, both back and front, had been prolonged and painstaking in the ensuing weeks.

'Put the whole of the garden down to vegetables, they have!' said Mrs Flynn censoriously.

'Why not?' answered Anna mildly. 'They've several children – they probably need lots of vegetables.'

'Letting the neighbourhood down,' snorted Mrs Flynn. 'We've all got a bit of lawn, and a bird bath, or a sundial or something nice. And she actually had washing out on a Sunday! It's so common!'

Anna made no reply.

'And despite that she takes a bag of washing to the launderette. You'd think with all those children she'd prefer to wash herself and save the money,' said Mrs Flynn spitefully.

'She probably has a very good reason,' said Anna firmly and Mrs Flynn subsided into self-righteous silence.

It was about this time that Tom Drew invited Anna to tea.

'I wish I could see the programme about wild animals tomorrow night,' she had said in the staff room one play-time, and was surprised to hear Tom's prompt reply.

'Come and see it at my digs. I've got a television set there. Come and have tea.'

'But what about your landlady –' Anna had faltered, thinking of Mrs Flynn's reaction if she had had such short notice of a visitor's arrival.

'She'll love it,' said Tom firmly; and thus it was settled.

Anna found his lodgings very much more comfortable than her own. The house was a solid Victorian structure, set in a garden thick with the evergreens so beloved by our great grandparents, about four miles west of Elm Hill along the old turnpike road.

As well as a bedroom, Tom had a small sitting-room which had once, Anna suspected, been the smoking den of a Victorian paterfamilias. She could imagine him sitting there, a century ago, at a great roll-top desk, a beaded smoking-cap upon his greying locks, going through the household accounts and wondering what on earth the housemaid did with all those candles and if she were really worth the five pounds per annum she was so fortunate in receiving.

Tom's landlady was a widow of majestic appearance who gave them tea in the drawing-room which ran the width of the house at the back. A verandah shadowed the room, but it was pleasant for Anna to see a matured garden in the dusk through its archways, after the bleak rawness of Mrs Flynn's surroundings.

She gave them hot buttered crumpets spread with 'Gentleman's Relish', wafer-thin bread and butter with home-made apple jelly, and generous slices of a fine dark plum cake which compared favourably with Anna's mother's prized recipe. Anna found herself enjoying it all immensely. To sit in a soft easy chair, with a long fire scorching one's legs, eating twice as much as usual, was extraordinarily pleasant after a day's teaching, and the contrast with her usual meal of a cup of tea, four Osborne biscuits or a dank thin slice of slab-cake served on a pseudo-Chinese metal tray by Mrs Flynn's grudging hand, made this richness all the more heart-warming.

It was plain that Mrs Armstrong was devoted to Tom. She kept a solicitous eye on his tea-cup, pressed her excellent food upon him, and generally spoilt him. Anna guessed that she had been brought up in a household where the men's comfort came first, and suspected that Tom made a very good substitute for the two sons who had recently married and left home.

'I'll see if your fire needs making up,' she said, rising to her feet.

'I'll do it,' said Tom, forestalling her, and vanishing towards his sitting-room. Mrs Armstrong smiled indulgently.

'He's really such a dear,' she confided to Anna. 'He's been with me over a year. So good-tempered and thoughtful.'

'I can imagine it,' said Anna.

'And so *clean*!' said Mrs Armstrong, with such emphasis, that Anna felt that no adequate answer could be made. It seemed rather an odd remark. Anna began to wonder whether Mrs Armstrong's own family had *not* been so clean, or whether Tom's use of hot water was unusually excessive and made too heavy demands upon an ancient plumbing system. She felt that it was a peculiar virtue to stress to a comparative stranger, and while she was turning over these thoughts in her mind Tom came back.

'I've put some logs on,' he said. Mrs Armstrong began to pack the tea things methodically upon the tea trolley.

'Then you must both go and watch your programme. It's almost time. I shall be here if you need me,' she added, with the slight formality of a chaperon, and dismissed them with a wave of the hand.

It was snug in Tom's little room and when the programme was over Anna was very content to sit smoking and talking companionably.

There was no doubt about it, Tom was a very reassuring person to be with. And uncommonly clean, thought Anna mischievously to herself. Looking at him in the firelight Anna

thought him almost handsome in an unobtrusive way. He wore good country clothes and was decidedly better groomed than his male colleagues at Elm Hill. Anna liked too his cheerful demeanour. He lacked the self-pity of Mr Foster and the arrogance of Andy Craig. Altogether she would have thought him very well settled in his job so that it was a shock when he said in the course of conversation:

'I'm thinking of leaving Elm Hill.'

'Why?' answered Anna. 'Don't you like teaching?'

'Do you?' he countered.

'I think so,' said Anna slowly. 'It's not a bit as I'd imagined it. I don't seem to have time to talk to the children individually – there are such masses of them and it makes me so tired I get cross unnecessarily. But I am liking it more as I go on. Yes, I think I'll really enjoy next term. But won't you?'

'No,' said Tom quietly. 'I'm in the wrong job and it's my own fault.'

'Tell me why,' asked Anna. There was a pause while Tom rearranged the logs. Bright flames licked up the chimney and lit up his young serious face.

'It's a fairly ordinary story, but I'll tell you if you really want to know.'

'Please,' said Anna.

'Well, my father owns a market garden between Cambridge and Bedford. It's wonderful soil – grows magnificent stuff – and he produces vegetables mainly and makes a reasonable living.' Anna noticed how his eyes lit up at the mention of the land. That's where his heart is, thought Anna, in a flash of insight.

'But it was pretty hard going in the early years. Both my father and mother were from large families. They both went to the same village school in the Fens, left at fourteen, and got married at twenty. I'm the only child and I'm afraid they've always thought far too much of me. Natural, I suppose, but as someone once said all children need a little "healthy neglect" which I never really had.'

'You don't appear spoilt now, if that's any comfort,' Anna assured him. Tom looked amused at her concern.

'They had very little money and both worked like beavers. I went to the grammar school near by and I helped on the home land whenever I could. After a superhuman effort my father managed to buy this market garden and I would love to work there too. But no!'

'Why not?'

'Not good enough for our son,' quoted Tom in mock solemnity. 'Can't have him soiling his hands after all that schooling. He must start higher up the ladder than we did. What else have we slaved for?'

'But if you *wanted* to – ' began Anna bewildered.

'Why didn't I say so?' finished Tom. 'Well, I did, in a half-hearted way, but they were so heart-broken at the idea and they'd always been so uncommonly good to me that I took the easy way out. I couldn't disappoint them. They'd set their hearts on my becoming a teacher, going on to college and bringing them credit – and so I just gave in.'

'And you're not happy?'

'I'm happy enough. I think I'd be happy anywhere. Life's pretty good, you know, wherever you find it. But I can't live without the country for ever and I'd dearly love to get back to some serious rose-growing.'

'Roses? Are they the first love?'

'They are,' said Tom enthusiastically. 'My father's started a few on the side, and they are exactly right for that soil! We could have a magnificent rose nursery in a few years there. I can't wait to start!'

'What will your parents say?'

Tom looked thoughtful.

'I don't think they'll mind so much now. I've done the college part and done some teaching. If they see I'm really determined to go back I think they'll be pleased eventually. In any case I should leave Elm Hill next summer and try for a country post.'

'You'd never get such a marvellous building,' pointed out Anna, remembering some of the rural schools in her own area.

'Not such an army in each class,' retorted Tom. 'That's what gets me down! It's not education. It's mass-pumping, and we get nowhere with it. Who wants a palace, so over-crowded that we have to be policemen, not teachers? I tell you, I'd rather go back to my old insanitary village school with two dozen in a class and a bit of humanity. At least we'd all have time and space to get to know each other!'

The young man spoke warmly and Anna realized that he had thought long and deeply about his job. He would be a sad loss to the school, and Anna felt a small pang of pain at the thought of his going. Not that she had had time to have much to do with him, but he seemed a right-thinking, cheerful young person, who knew what he wanted of life and was now intent upon getting it.

She had food for thought as they went back to Mrs Flynn's together. They said good-bye at the gate and as Tom's footsteps receded up the road, Anna looked forlornly at the struggling lilac bush, the twigs of privet, and the six dead geraniums still planted in the centre bed cut in the sparse new grass.

If this was the best town could offer, thought Anna, fumbling for her key, she didn't blame Tom for returning to the country! Whichever he chose to raise, roses or country pupils, he would be engaged in creating something worthwhile in conditions already far more heartening than those at Elm Hill.

Feeling suddenly rebellious against life in general – too many children to teach, Tom's plan for leaving, the petty meanness of the detestable Mrs Flynn – Anna slammed the front door, made the loathsome little house shudder, and went crossly to bed.

9. Plays and Pipe Dreams

THE bustle of Christmas preparations at school worked the children into a state of seething excitement. They ran faster, talked more, slammed doors, scattered blots from pens shaking with excitement, turned over two pages instead of one, fidgeted and twisted and turned in a fever of impatience, starry-eyed, for the glory that was to come.

Anna, her own young spirits rising, could not help sympathizing with their ecstasy, but found teaching them doubly hard. She became cunning at adapting any lesson to the subject of Christmas, using their boundless energy to further the preparations. To attempt anything alien to this all-conquering force was asking for blood, sweat, and tears, and Anna bowed to the inevitable.

They read about Christmas, wrote about Christmas, made up sums about lengths of paper-chains, the cost of presents, the height of Christmas trees, and the length of stockings. The afternoons were devoted to rehearsals for the Christmas concert, the practising of carols, and the eager construction of Christmas presents and cards for their families.

Anna watched them one afternoon at their card-making, amused by the variety of methods and materials they had chosen. Outside the leaden sky lowered over sullen, cold fields, but in the classroom the lights shone down upon children painting, children cutting out bright gummed paper with energetic scissors, children tapping frenziedly at snow scenes with agitated pencils, and children absorbed in unusually tidy lettering.

In the front desk sat George and Peter, hard at work. George was a large, stolid, slow-moving child, no match for his skinny volatile neighbour who kept up a running commentary on his actions. It was in keeping with George's nature that he should have chosen to paint, with a fine brush, an elaborate scene of a village inn and a stage-coach complete with four horses in intricate harness. His paint-brush moved slowly and laboriously, his tongue writhing from his mouth as he concentrated.

Beside him Peter had elected to cut out some dashing Christmas trees from gummed paper. They were done quickly he knew and would look effective. He chattered brightly to his labouring companion as he folded his own first piece of green paper, and began slashing dramatically with his scissors.

'This won't take no time, George! Bet I get six done before you've half finished that old thing!' The scissors flashed and triangles of green paper fell swiftly upon the desk.

'Six'll just do nicely,' continued Peter. 'Mum and Dad, and five aunties. How many do you want?'

George sighed heavily.

'Ten really, but I don't expect I'll have the time.' He bent again to his task and began to paint carefully the spokes of the coach wheels. Smugly his companion opened out a beautiful Christmas tree, applied a wet tongue to its back and banged it firmly down upon his folded paper.

'There!' he said triumphantly. 'One done!' George cast a morose glance upon it, but said nothing.

'I might put a setting sun or a robin or something up the corner,' meditated the irrepressible Peter, head on one side. 'Got plenty of time,' he added maddeningly.

He counted five pieces of green paper, stacked them together, and folded them over busily, thumping joyously with a small grubby fist. George began to outline the harness. The bells were going to be uncommonly tricky to manoeuvre.

'This way,' exulted Peter, 'I can cut the whole lot out at once. Won't be no time at all. Here, you'd best get a move on with all that lot to do. Bet you don't get *one* finished this lesson.'

George remained silent, but by the tightening of his lips

Anna could see that this goading was almost more than he could bear. Had he been working alone his slow-growing masterpiece would have delighted him, but the boasting mass-producer at his side wrecked all his own pleasures of creation. He plied his careful brush diligently but sadly.

Beside him Peter gave a sudden yelp of dismay. In each hand he held the fringed remnants of five decimated Christmas trees, and his face was growing slowly scarlet.

'Look at that now!' said the mass-producer, vexed. 'I've been and cut through the fold!'

A smile of infinite satisfaction spread slowly across George's countenance. With a happy sigh he raised his brush and set briskly to work upon the horses' tails.

The Christmas concert was to take place on the last two afternoons of term, for the hall was not large enough to accommodate all the parents at one performance.

A staff meeting was called about a month or so before the dates arranged in order to decide the programme. Anna sat on a hard chair at the uncomfortably crowded long table and watched Miss Enderby at the end. The headmistress gazed at them speculatively over the top of her half-glasses, tapping her pen rhythmically on the paper before her.

'Shall we take it class by class or jot down suggestions as they occur to us?' she asked.

'Suggestions!'

'Yes, suggestions!'

'Suggestions, by all means!' chorused the older members of staff emphatically, to Anna's surprise. She was soon to learn the reason for their unwonted unity.

Miss Hobbs was first to speak.

'I'll take ball games to music,' she announced firmly. 'If that seems suitable,' she added, as a concession to politeness.

'Perfectly suitable,' said Miss Enderby, scribbling smoothly. 'Ball games – Miss Hobbs. Any other ideas?'

'The Mad Hatter's Tea Party,' said Joan Berry promptly. Miss Enderby's pen flowed on.

'Carols and a tableau,' said Mr Foster, before she had finished writing 'Tea Party'.

'Mimed nursery rhymes,' whispered a mole.

'Percussion band,' whispered the other. Their whispers overlapped and Miss Enderby's pen quickened its pace.

Anna began to feel quite bewildered. All the best ideas were being snaffled with incredible ruthlessness. The others must have been thinking things up for weeks! What on earth could her class do? Music, plays, mimes had all been whisked away before her startled eyes. What else was there? She began groping murkily about the corners of her brain. Her children were particularly quick and agile. Perhaps something to do with gymnastics?

As she fumbled with her thoughts, feeling as slow-witted as George among a number of adult Peters, Tom Drew spoke up.

'We'll have a go at gymnastics of some sort – somersaults, that sort of thing. I thought perhaps a street scene with tumblers and clowns. We could disguise the piano as an outsize barrel-organ perhaps?'

Anna could have killed him, sitting there looking so deferential and innocent, watching his suggestion being inscribed on the fast-filling sheet of paper. As slick and ruthless and self-seeking as the rest! thought Anna rebelliously, seeing her only hope whisked so neatly away from her. She fell to searching the empty cupboard of her mind yet again as the smug, bright voices echoed around her and Miss Enderby's pen scampered down the list nineteen to the dozen.

'The King's Breakfast.'

'Royalties,' said someone importantly. 'Quite impossible!'

'Oh, fiddlesticks! We did it at Brownies last year and I'm positive no mention was made of royalties!'

'Put the babies down for "Christmas Fairies – A Dance".'

'We'll have a go with our recorders!'

Anna began to feel more and more helpless. Miss Enderby's pen slowed to a stop and remained poised.

'Anyone not settled?' she asked. Her glance, bright and appraising, flashed round her staff who had so efficiently acquitted themselves that only a bare twenty minutes had been needed for the concert arrangements so far.

'Me,' said Anna, in a small voice.

Everyone turned to stare at her. A number of people spoke at once. Tongues clicked with concern.

'Miss Lacey!'

'Poor dear! Now, let's think!'

'Haven't you any ideas at all?'

'What about a little play?'

'We've already got three, dear.'

'What about singing?'

'What about dancing?'

'What about a novelty number?'

A novelty number! scoffed Anna indignantly to herself. And what might that repellent name cover? She gazed round at their faces, perturbed, thoughtful, helpful and concerned, but each wearing a suspicion of smug superiority to Anna's jaundiced eyes.

'But you must have *some* idea of what your class can do,' Miss Enderby said, with a hint of impatience in her voice. It was really most annoying for a woman priding herself on her responsive staff – a credit to her own superb staff-handling – to be held up by a stupid little girl who could think of nothing for herself.

'They can do somersaults and things,' faltered Anna weakly, 'and I was going to suggest something like Mr Drew's idea –'

'Then you do that,' said Tom promptly, 'and I'll do a skit on "What's My Line". Come to think of it, I'd sooner do that.'

Anna could have shaken him. It was quite bad enough to have had her first idea frightened into the open by Miss Enderby's impatience. Now she felt a rat as well as an idiot. And how infuriating of Tom to be so maddeningly magnanimous and so bursting with ideas into the bargain! But the faces were still turned towards her, smiling and relieved, and common civility must be served. She turned a grateful smile upon Tom.

'It's very nice of you. Are you sure?'

'Positive,' said Tom cheerfully. 'I'd really prefer "What's My Line". Those somersault acts have to be really good to come off.'

Anna, still quivering with all she had endured, drew in a breath. Tom cast her a quick sideways glance and seemed to feel that something more should be added to his last remark.

'Yours will do it all splendidly!' he assured her hastily. 'And what's more, I'll thread the piano with paper for you so that it sounds like a real barrel-organ!'

Softened by such generosity Anna's rage melted away, and she was able to throw herself with renewed zest into the crazy discussion of ways and means of making the Christmas con-cert the biggest success that Elm Hill had ever known.

Rehearsals went on to the accompaniment of thunderous activity from the school field where the new infants' block was rising rapidly. Besides the cement mixer's throaty growl, the noise of lorries, the scream of drills, the sibilant swish of stone and gravel rushing from tip-up vehicles, the clanging of metal scaffolding, and the glad cries of several dozen workmen all made Anna's voice inaudible to the children. A near-by airfield added its quota of screaming jets to the pandemonium and Anna, at times, was forced to write her more urgent directions on the blackboard and tap lustily at them with a pointer until she had her class's attention.

This was one of the things that her college mentors had omitted to tell her. There had never been any mention of noise in her teaching duties. If anything, noise had only been spoken of as something rather desirable in class working time.

'Those dreadful, dreadful days,' Anna remembered her frail white-haired Education Lecturer saying, 'when children were told to listen to a pin drop, and to be seen and not heard! What repressed silent classes I remember seeing – little mouths shut, little fingers locked together in laps, not a sound or movement allowed! Remember, ladies, a happy busy noise means a happy, busy class.'

Anna, at times, longed for a return to those 'dreadful, dreadful days'.

She realized that more than half the racket came from outside, but even so, her exuberant class made plenty of fuss on their own. She took to having short 'silent periods' when the children must work without speaking, and these not only saved her reason but, she found, were the times when the class did its best, tidiest, and most thoughtful work. It was about time, thought Anna, watching a duffle-coated architect balancing on a plank high up on the new building, that schools were built with sound-proof walls. Any noise inside then would be legitimate and under control. It was hopeless to expect children, and adults too for that matter, to concentrate amidst such a fury of sound. She comforted herself in those last hectic weeks of term with the thought of the quiet countryside awaiting her and the blissful all-embracing silence of the widespread sleeping fields.

Meanwhile the staff room was a haven of peace, for this was on the side of the school furthest from the builders' activities, and, mercifully, the numbers present were fewer.

Anna shared it with Alan Foster for one period a week when their free time overlapped. He had sent off the children's book, he told Anna, and was now busy with another effort.

Anna looked at his bald head, across which the sparse hair was so carefully and evenly arranged in seven parallel lines with an inch of pink scalp showing between each, and wondered what new brain-child had been born within that striped bony box.

'I've been thinking about our last conversation, you know. About text-books. I think you may be right and that they are not such a good bet after all.'

'I'm afraid I've forgotten,' confessed Anna. But she need not have feared that Mr Foster's feelings were hurt. He was much too engrossed in his new venture.

'It's reference books that are needed now! Take our own classrooms. What are the books most in use with our top class juniors?'

Anna thought, rightly, that this question was purely rhetorical and remained silent.

'Why, the encyclopedias!' exclaimed Alan Foster, thumping his hand on the table and making the marking pencils jump. 'And the dictionaries! And the reference books! "Go and look it up, boy," we say when anyone wants to know what a coelacanthus is! That's the thing to cash in on these days.'

His moist eyes fairly flashed with enthusiasm and Anna felt like a mother depriving a baby of its bottle when she said:

'But will you have the time? And won't you need an awful lot of real knowledge?'

Alan Foster's flabby face crumpled a little, but his voice remained enthusiastic.

'Plenty of other people get by and make a packet. Don't see why I shouldn't be able to do the same. Besides, I've plenty of friends I could get to do a bit of looking up for me.'

'But it isn't just a case of "making a packet" and "getting people to look up things",' insisted Anna. She felt cross and helpless and annoyed with herself for bothering to sound like a Sunday School teacher, but was determined to make her point. 'A reference book is something to rely on, something of value, something of integral worth. You can't just fling a few vague facts together – simply in the hope of raising money – when people will be *relying* on the work you are doing.'

'Oh, I can see that,' replied Alan Foster airily. But Anna knew that he did not see and was not capable of seeing. There he sat, a vast, crumpled, mountain of a man, spattered with cigarette ash, too lazy even to think straightforwardly.

'You'd do better to stop smoking, if you're short of money,' said Anna downrightly, 'than sit wasting the school's time and your own on a lot of hare-brained schemes that won't come off!'

As soon as she had said it Anna was appalled. Anyone would think I was his wife, thought Anna! She began to rush in with gabbled apologies.

'I'm most terribly sorry. I shouldn't have spoken so rudely. Please –' she started.

Alan Foster turned a mild face upon her.

'Don't apologize, my dear. Actually, for a youngster you talk quite a lot of sense.' He fumbled for a cigarette in a squashed packet and lit it meditatively.

'I can't give this up,' he said, blowing a blue cloud, 'but I think perhaps the reference book might be a little too much for me. Besides, I'd have to offer my friends part of the profits, if they'd given me a hand.'

He's absolutely incorrigible! thought Anna. Afraid of giving way to another spasm of frankness, which she would later regret, she rose to put on the kettle ready for playtime tea.

'What about an anthology?' said Alan Foster, raising his voice above Anna's clatterings. 'No work at all, to speak of.'

He puffed thoughtfully, his eyes already brightening to that moist fanatic ambience which Anna was beginning to recognize as yet another sign of wish-fulfilment.

'My brother wrote several books, you know,' he added conversationally. 'Did I ever tell you?'

'Yes,' said Anna. She felt like adding, 'Several times,' but bit it back. There was no point in prodding this cloudy mass. No impression could be made.

'He got up an anthology. Modern poets, I think it was. Friends of his wrote poetry in those days.'

'Did it pay?' asked Anna bitterly, tinkling teaspoons into saucers with furious speed.

'No,' said Alan Foster, in sudden surprise. 'Come to think of it, it didn't. In fact, I believe he paid half the cost of publishing.' He sighed heavily.

In the distance the bell shrilled and the sound of children's voices could be heard. There was a clatter of footsteps outside the door as the staff flocked tea-wards.

'So that won't do,' sighed Alan Foster, piling up his unmarked books. 'What do you suggest now, young lady?'

'Please yourself,' said Anna shortly.

'They're putting the door frames in the new buildings,' said Joan Berry, between sips of near-boiling tea.

'Might get the infants in there by Easter, at this rate,' said Andy Craig.

'Ought to see the advertisement for a headmistress in the *Teacher's World* any day now,' said Tom Drew, dropping four lumps carefully into his cup. 'Going to try for it, Anna?'

'No, thanks,' answered Anna. 'I can't keep forty-odd in order, let alone four hundred.'

Andy Craig looked hastily round the staff room and seeing only five present, dropped his voice conspiratorially.

'La Belle Flo has her great luscious teeth bared to grab this juicy bone, I hear. And, what's more, she's just offered her services to the Deprived Persons' Movement which is Councillor Ormond's pet project at the moment.'

Councillor Ormond was head of the managers of Elm Hill School, but Andy's mysterious nods and winks, as he disclosed his news, had no significance for Anna. Joan Berry, however, had something to add.

'But Councillor Ormond does not like dear Flo, as you should know, my boy. They don't wear the same coloured rosettes on election day. Personally I back Marjorie Jennings.'

'Marjorie Jennings!' exploded Alan Foster. 'Why, she's ten years younger than I am!'

'Well?' asked Joan coolly.

'Well, it's just absurd! A chit of a girl like that –'

'Some chit,' said Tom Drew unchivalrously. 'Must weigh thirteen stone at least.'

'She seems a chit to me,' maintained Alan Foster. '*And* a flibbertigibbet! Always was. Made no secret of the fact she went to Goldsmiths' for her training so that she could see plenty of the opposite sex.' He puffed out his flabby cheeks crossly.

'I was there some time before,' he added, and looked vaguely surprised at their laughter.

'If the appointments board has any sense at all it will choose a stranger,' said Tom Drew. 'There are about a dozen eligibles in this area, all as green as grass with jealousy, as far as I can make out. One of them told me on the bus this morning the past histories of two of her rivals she's known since schooldays here. It's a wonder they're not either in prison or a mental home, if all I heard was true. And what's more,' said Tom, putting his cup on the tray, 'it's a marvel *she's* not up for defamation of character.'

He shook his dark head sadly, and looked with mock seriousness at Anna.

'My, my!' he moralized. 'What ugly passions ambition doth let loose, to be sure!'

10. Country Christmas

THE solid comfort of the Essex farmhouse was bliss to Anna after the box-like frailty and pokiness of her lodgings. Here was companionship, warmth and laughter. Besides the voices of her parents and the two young brothers home from school the house itself whispered to her in a dozen different ways. The fire crackled, the kettle sizzled, the old doors squeaked on their ancient hinges, and a loose flagstone in the hall gave a cheerful and familiar thump to the hurrying feet. It was all exactly as it should be, and Anna felt her old self again.

She had arrived at the end of term very much tireder than she realized. Small presents had been exchanged among the staff that last morning and the children had brought cards and handkerchiefs and tiny bottles of potent scent and bright pink soap and Anna had suddenly felt overwhelmingly fond of them all – even Arnold.

Most of the staff were spending Christmas with their families, but the moles, surprisingly enough, were setting off to Austria for winter sports and were almost gay with this unwonted excitement.

Miss Hobbs, answering Anna's civil inquiries about her holiday plans, flushed an unbecoming red and said that she had enrolled for a ten-day course on the teaching of infants.

'Must look ahead, you know. And if Miss Enderby gets her deserts I should like to be by her side.'

'Naturally,' said Anna, trying to hide her astonishment.

'And not a word, please, to the others, dear,' begged Miss Hobbs. 'Nothing may come of our plans. No need to broadcast all one's doing.'

Anna had promised to say nothing, though she did not think it mattered very much if Miss Hobbs's ambitions were known.

After all, she was quite at liberty to go on a course, and not many of the staff would be so loyal as to give up most of their holiday for the problematical future welfare of their head-mistress.

Anna was relieved to be away from them all and to slip back into the ways of home. It was a relief not to have to guard one's tongue, for Miss Hobbs's last-minute confidence was only one of dozens Anna had heard that term, but to be able to chatter and rag with the boys as they rampaged about the house busy putting up Christmas decorations. It was a relief not to worry about people's feelings, about using someone else's coat-hanger, or tea-cup, or unwittingly borrowing someone else's book. Above all, it was a relief to be with a few people in a large space for a change, and to know that no matter how much noise they made it could never be as shattering and as nerve-racking as the din at Elm Hill School.

During the cheerful bustle of Christmas preparations her father told her that he was taking on a farming pupil. He would come to live with them on the first of January.

'Do I know him?' asked Anna, busy chopping apples for fruit salad on the great kitchen table.

'Should do,' said her father. 'Edward Marchant's boy. Young Edward.'

'I thought he'd taken up engineering,' said Anna. She wrinkled her brows in heavy thought. Young Edward Marchant – a tall gangling boy whom she had met at local parties and youthful dancing classes – yes, she remembered him vaguely. The Marchants farmed a dozen or so miles away on the Suffolk border.

'He didn't take to it,' answered her father. 'He's going on to Cirencester or one of those agricultural places – can't remember which now, though Ted did tell me. Anyway, he's got to get his practical work in, and as Ted asked me I was only too pleased to have the lad. Nice family. He'll fit in here. Makes more work for your mother though, Anna, I'm afraid.'

'We've had pupils before,' said Anna comfortably, 'so I don't expect she'll mind.'

'She was younger then,' said her father. Anna felt a pang. Somehow one never thought of mothers getting old. Other people's mothers did, of course, but one's own always seemed the same age. She stopped chopping for a moment to consider this phenomenon.

'You'll have to make it up to her in some way,' said Anna, after a pause. 'She could do with a little car of her own instead of that ramshackle old Land Rover.'

She had said the words in jest, but watched, with growing delight, her father's slow smile.

'By George!' he exclaimed, 'that's an idea! I'll think about that one, Anna. She could bob off for her shopping whenever she liked without having to come running after me for the Land Rover.'

He walked up and down the kitchen, jingling the coins in his trousers' pocket and pondering Anna's suggestion. Suddenly he stopped and turned a radiant face towards her.

'It would be jolly useful too to pull a little trailer on market days. Just the thing for a few hens or piglets. I must certainly think about this!' He hurried out into the farmyard.

'Men!' said his daughter disgustedly to the empty kitchen.

The village church, on Christmas Day, was aglow with candles, berried holly, and Christmas roses. The silver on the altar gleamed from Miss Fuller's ministrations, for she would allow no other hand to touch it. As Anna knew, the church silver was probably Miss Fuller's only real interest in life. She lived alone, on a modest income, and had admitted to Anna once, in a burst of mouse-like confidence, that she felt quite useless. Only the cleaning of the church silver gave her the feeling of being of any use to the small community, and to see her bearing it to her small cottage near by, in a clothes basket each Saturday morning, was a heart-warming and familiar sight to her neighbours.

The vicar was in his most festive robes. He gleamed with gold thread and rich embroidery as he mounted the steps to the pulpit and Anna soon found her attention wandering as his light amiable voice fluttered its way to his unusually numerous congregation. He was a happy man, an exception to the usual run of people, thought Anna, remembering Alan Foster, Florence Enderby, Mrs Flynn, and the other odd fish of Elm Hill.

Perhaps he lacked ambition, mused Anna, and so enjoyed life as it came. Ambition, she was beginning to think, was a two-edged weapon. It could provide a motive, an interest, a spur. It could be the means of living in a state of perpetual hope. She thought of Miss Hobbs at her infants' course and of Miss Fuller at her determined silver-cleaning.

But on the other hand it could lead to self-aggrandisement and self-deception. She remembered Mrs Flynn's patronizing airs to her neighbour, and Alan Foster's literary aspirations which would never be fulfilled, and his boastings about his brother's eminence, which Anna found pitiful.

'And now to God the Father' floated from the pulpit, and Anna rose to her feet feeling uncommonly guilty, for not a word of the good vicar's homily had reached her.

But, as she greeted friends outside, she was conscious of a feeling of well-being within her and could only suppose that, by a process akin to osmosis, she had drawn in spiritual grace from her lovely surroundings.

Young Edward Marchant arrived on New Year's Day and Anna was amazed to see how massive he had grown. He towered over her tall father, his face was plump and bronzed as a pumpkin, and his hearty voice outdid those of her vociferous young brothers. These two were delighted to welcome this addition to the household and followed him about the farm marvelling at his easy strength.

'Ted lifted two sacks at a time!' gasped one with admiration.

'He carried that five-barred gate from the paddock to the stable,' said the other with awe.

Patrick Lacey certainly seemed to be lucky in his pupil. He was cheerful, willing, as strong as a horse, and eager to learn. In the house he proved himself considerate and tidy, and Margaret Lacey found herself growing very fond of him as the days passed. His prodigious appetite was a joy to her motherly heart and a challenge to her cooking prowess. It soon became a source of good-natured teasing by the Lacey family and 'Ted'll finish it up!' became a byword.

Although he was in boisterous good spirits with Anna's brothers, and natural and at ease with her parents, with Anna herself he seemed unusually shy at first. He had no sisters, she knew, and guessed that this might be the reason for his formality with her, and did her best to appear as welcoming as she could.

There was plenty of work on the farm to keep all the men busy, for early lambs were arriving thick and fast. The weather had turned cold, after a mild Christmas, with a wicked north-easter that shrivelled the grass and battered the rows of wall-flowers that lined the path to the farmhouse.

One cold afternoon Anna took the pile of Christmas cards, which had decorated the house, to Miss Anderson at the village school. She had taken the used Christmas cards each year, for as far back as she could remember, and the children used them for classroom friezes, calendars, blotters, scrap-books, and all manner of things.

This year she had gone through the cards with unusual care and had selected a number for her own class's edification before setting out on the mile-long walk to the village.

It was not an inspiring day. This truly was the dead of the year. The black hedges stood stiff and splintery with the cold, the wind shrilling through their tracery. Dust and dry leaves

eddied at the side of the lane, and small birds were blown sideways on the slip-stream of gusty wind. Anna clutched the parcel
painfully to her chest, head down and eyes streaming. With
the other hand she beat upon her thigh to engender some
warmth. There was no doubt about it, there would be snow
before long, thought Anna, country wise.

Miss Anderson's schoolroom was a pleasant haven from the
cold. An open fire roared behind a large fireguard and a half
circle of children sat round it listening to *The Tailor of Gloucester*. Their faces were rosy from the heat and most of them had
stretched their slippered feet towards the blaze. Anna noticed
a row of outdoor shoes warming comfortably, ready for home
time, and thought how cosily domestic it all seemed compared
with Elm Hill's bleak cloakrooms and classrooms.

Next door she could hear the infants singing, and beyond
the partition the only other class, which was the top one,
appeared to be listening to a B.B.C. schools' programme.

Miss Anderson had been head teacher for years at the village
school and Anna always enjoyed her visits there, but this time

she looked with new interest at the little group in her charge. She knew almost all of them. There were the eight-year-old twins – sons of her father's shepherd – children from the Post Office and the grocer's shop, from farms in the neighbourhood, and houses in the village itself. They all looked as healthy as her own high-spirited young villains, she thought, but were considerably more docile. Perhaps Miss Anderson's years of teaching had something to do with it. Or maybe, she decided more ruefully, it is easier to have a spirit of serenity in a gathering of eighteen rather than forty-six.

She accepted Miss Anderson's invitation to sit and warm herself, and the children eagerly brought her a chair and shifted round to give her a central position in front of the blaze.

Miss Anderson seated herself again at the side of the hearth, book in hand, and resumed the story. Anna sat as quietly engrossed as her small neighbours as the tale unwound. With Christmas still fresh in their minds, the story of that distant snowy Gloucester where the poor old tailor tossed feverishly in his four-poster, while the sound of bells filled the narrow streets, gripped these young listeners. They tut-tutted over the wickedness of Simpkin the cat, and their sympathy, Anna was amused to see, was wholly for the mice. Simpkin's hunger was all that he deserved, it seemed to them.

They leant forward eagerly to see the beautiful little pictures as Miss Anderson held out the book for them to see. How lovely, thought Anna, to be able to show the whole class such minute illustrations without moving from one's chair! At Elm Hill she would have been forced to walk slowly round the room, letting a few at a time see the treasures, while the others fidgeted with impatience or lost interest altogether.

Yes, despite the drawbacks of Miss Anderson's village school, the dark old-fashioned building, the primitive and distant sanitation, the comparative paucity of stock which made Anna's Christmas cards all the more welcome, and the great range of age in each class, still Miss Anderson had one price-less advantage.

Her class was small, and each individual in it was known to her as if he were her own flesh and blood; known far more intimately than ever Anna could hope to know her own large brood at Elm Hill, despite the laudable efforts of the Parent–Teacher association.

She felt suddenly and insanely envious of Miss Anderson. There she sat, grey-haired, wrinkled, wrapped in a green stuff frock that was four years old and unfashionably long. The small hands that held the book were chapped and grubby from keeping the great fire fed, and her thin voice was cracked with much use. But she was a good teacher and her children returned the affection and care she gave them. They all, it seemed, had time for one another; and Anna envied her luck in having a family around her, spinster though she was.

At Elm Hill, Anna knew, the size of her class precluded any such family feeling, and thinking of next term in that chilly overcrowded palace, Anna relished the flickering firelight in the darkening schoolroom as a happy anachronism, and won-dered, for the first time, if such little schools would still be found in the English countryside when she had served her apprenticeship and felt free to choose her own place.

11. Joan's Parasite

THE walls of the new school had leapt up several feet when Anna returned, and already the gaunt framework of the roof was outlined against the sky.

It was to be a building of one storey and from Anna's high window she could now see how extensively it spread. Under the skeleton roof she watched the workmen and the duffle-coated architect thread their way along embryo corridors and into future classrooms still open to the blustering winds and unkind January skies. Her headmistress too, she noticed, made her way to the classroom windows, whenever she had occasion to call upon her, and stood gazing reflectively upon the scene of her hopes.

There was a speculative gleam in Florence Enderby's eye these days, which did not escape her staff's attention, and her public activities had increased tenfold.

She was in attendance at the Civic Ball, charity concerts, and innumerable public meetings held under the pinnacled roof of Elm Hill Town Hall; and all sorts of plans for opening her own school to the general public, as well as the pupils' parents, filled her staff with alarm tempered with amusement.

'Flo's publicity campaign,' Joan Berry remarked tartly to Anna one day, 'is going to make this place unbearable. She's just told me – politely of course – that I might be more comfortable in a fuller skirt. "Those side-slits, dear, must be draughty in this weather!"' Joan mimicked her headmistress's pontifical tones with cruel accuracy.

'I've been told to take down two wall pictures with torn corners,' observed Andy Craig, adjusting the spotted silk sling which had replaced the wrist strap during this term. 'I was told they looked slovenly.'

'Mark my words,' said Joan, 'there'll be an almighty blitz on us all until this confounded appointment's made. We'll have to face parents and all the local educational big-wigs flocking through the classrooms to see what a marvel dear Flo is.'

'Let's hope she gets it,' said Andy Craig. 'Life here won't be worth living if she doesn't. I think I'd go back in the R.A.F., if it weren't for this!'

He waved the sling bravely, winced creditably, and gave a sidelong look at Anna to see if she had noticed. Much to her annoyance, she had.

The weather continued to be bitterly cold. The muddy rutted roads were as hard as concrete and the wire netting which divided the new gardens was rimmed throughout each leaden day with whiskers of frost.

It was now that the flimsy shoddiness of Mrs Flynn's house was exposed. Wicked draughts blew under ill-fitting doors and the tiled bathroom was like a refrigerator. Condensed steam ran steadily to the floor from the chilly walls and the ventilator, already rusting high in the wall, emitted a thin scream as the wind whistled across the surrounding marshland and forced its way through the aperture.

Anna, despite a hot water bottle and a meagre smelly oil heater provided grudgingly by Mrs Flynn, could not get warm in her bedroom. The mattress was thin, and the blankets heavy but largely of cotton and smelling dismally of dog-biscuits. A lumpy eiderdown, which Mrs Flynn unearthed at Anna's timid request, added its quota of moth-ball perfume to the general unsavouriness. The weekends, in a house with two-feet thick brick walls, massive fires, and a snug bed, grew doubly precious at this time of year.

At school the children sniffed and coughed and rubbed chilblained toes and fingers. They disliked going out to play in the freezing playground and huddled, hiding, in the cloakrooms or lavatories. They became liverish and irritable, and the brisk north-easter did nothing to relive their discomfort.

In the staff room Alan Foster displayed, with misplaced pride, a hideous cold of gargantuan proportions.

'I'b an absolute bartyre to codes,' he told the assembled company one playtime.

'You should really be in bed,' scolded Miss Hobbs.

'Card leab all the work for you good beople to do,' said Alan Foster nobly. A shattering sneeze escaped him before he could find his damp handkerchief. After several earsplitting convulsions he stood helplessly in their midst turning his bleary streaming eyes from one to the other and drawing in great gulps of air through his flabby mouth.

'Oh dear! So sorry!' he moaned thickly. His colleagues, edging back, looked at him with dislike.

'No business to be here, giving us all your germs,' said Joan Berry roundly, voicing the private feelings of them all. 'Why on earth don't you go home?'

'She's right, old chap,' said Andy Craig. 'Sorry to lose you and all that, but we'd sooner have your class than your cold – to put it brutally.'

Alan Foster gave him a cold watery glance.

'I'b nod in the habit,' he said, with ponderous dignity, 'of givig ub by job for a cobbod code. I'b still capable of teaching I hobe.'

'You're a mutton-headed old chump,' said Tom Drew, 'and a walking menace into the bargain.'

But he said it affectionately, and as he passed Mr Foster's indignant bulk on the way to the door he gave him a clap on the shoulder which appeared to comfort the sufferer.

It was during this bleak period that Anna was invited to Joan Berry's flat for the evening.

She lived nearer town, about five miles from Elm Hill, in a prosperous and pleasant suburb where lime trees shaded the broad pavements in summer and twinkling gas lamps threw a welcoming beam upon tall evergreens and solid gateposts in winter.

Joan's flat was one of three in a comfortable red brick house set back from a quiet road. A little lantern with amber glass shed a warm glow over the deep porch as Anna waited, stamping her feet to keep them from freezing.

Joan was a cheering sight when she opened the door. She wore a bright red frock, unadorned with jewellery, which showed up her dark good looks. Anna followed her elegant legs and stiletto heels up the shallow stairs and marvelled at the warmth which enveloped the house.

A fire crackled and sparkled in the grate in Joan's sitting-room, and to Anna's surprise, a young man rose from an armchair beside it.

'This is Maurice Long,' said Joan, 'an old friend of mine. Unfortunately, he can't be with us for long, but we've time to have a drink together.'

The young man, Anna thought, looked a little put out by these words, but he smiled pleasantly enough and busied himself with preparing the drinks for Joan. He was small and very fair, with the girlish good looks which would lapse, later in life, to tubby dapperness. His manner was deprecating and Anna felt that he stood in some awe of Joan to whom he occasionally gave a fleeting glance of apprehension.

'Maurice has been working at a travel agency,' said Joan, nodding towards a pile of vivid leaflets which lay on the floor, 'and I've been torturing myself trying to choose a summer holiday.'

'Portugal!' said Maurice, firmly. 'It's quite perfect – and not outrageously expensive.'

'Oily cooking,' said Joan.

'Where have you planned to go?' asked Maurice, refilling Anna's glass neatly.

'Well, I suppose it will be Devon again,' said Anna. It sounded very unadventurous and she sought to justify such mediocrity. 'You see, my father can't get away in August, because of the harvest – he's a farmer. And my mother takes this little cottage and my brothers and I seem to go every year.'

'It sounds charming,' said Maurice with polite enthusiasm. 'Did you say your father farmed? Are there any openings in farming?'

Anna looked at his delicate hands and willowy figure, and wondered how he would fare at baling on a scorching August day, or if he could push his way, buckets in hand, through a milling mob of hefty hungry pigs in a muddy pig pen. She thought of Ted, her father's pupil, who would make two of the slight young man before her.

'Have you done any farming?' she asked cautiously.

'No. No, indeed. But there appears to be a great deal of money in it these days. And it must be a wonderfully healthy life. And I gather that the things one can slide on to the expenses account are legion. I must say it all sounds most attractive.'

'It's usual to have some practical experience first,' said Anna, ignoring the temptation to debate the financial side of farming. 'Then of course you could go on to an agricultural college for your training.'

Maurice laughed lightly and looked at Joan.

'Afraid I'm a bit long in the tooth for such things. Besides I'm an orphan boy and must earn while I learn.'

'It's almost seven o'clock,' said Joan pointedly.

There was an uncomfortable little silence. Maurice's weak mouth took on an almost mutinous line and Anna wondered what the mystery was.

'I'm not at all sure – ' he began, in a voice rather high with tension.

'Maurice!' said Joan. Her voice was low and steady. It held a hint of appeal as well as warning. 'You promised, you know.'

'Oh, very well,' said Maurice pettishly. He put his empty

glass on the tray and braced himself. His face was thunderous, but he did his best to smile at Anna as he bade her farewell.

'Have you got the key?' asked Joan to his departing back. Maurice hit his pockets rapidly and then nodded.

At the door he turned, and looking rather ashamed, addressed Joan.

'Good-bye, dear. Don't wait up. I may be late.'

As the door closed behind him Joan let forth a sigh of relief, blowing smoke ceilingwards.

'Poor dear!' she said affectionately. 'I didn't think he'd go, you know!'

'Where is he going?' asked Anna, as Joan seemed to be inclined to confide.

'To the Youth Club. I help there twice a week and Maurice has been coming with me while he's been here. Tom Drew comes now and again and teaches the boys to box.'

She rose to replenish the fire with small logs and Anna was glad that she could not see her astonishment. That the glamorous Joan Berry, whom Anna had dismissed as an attractive but quite selfish person, should give up two evenings a week to Youth Club work was a distinct shock to the unsophisticated countrygirl. She had never been inside a Youth Club herself and had vague impressions of tough Teddy boys and tougher Teddy girls jiving and jeering, between bouts of bottle-throwing and impassioned love-making. She looked at Joan with new respect.

She felt, too, extremely curious about the relationship between her hostess and Maurice Long. It seemed odd, to say the least of it, to hear Maurice announcing that he would be staying the night when, as Anna knew, there was only one bedroom containing Joan's single bed, in the little flat. Anna hoped she wasn't prudish, but it was not the sort of situation she met with in her own home background, and the blood of generations of upright East Anglians beat steadily in her veins. Somehow one didn't think of teachers – well – living in sin.

She gazed, perplexed, at the dancing flames and Joan Berry, glancing at her pink bewildered face, smiled and told her more.

'Maurice is living here for a bit.' She gave a laugh, bubbling with amusement. 'Don't think, dear child, that he is living *with* me: Perish the thought! The dear boy sleeps chastely and rather uncomfortably, I suspect – on that couch over there. But he really is an old friend. I've known him since he was six and he fell off a punt at Pangbourne at the same picnic.'

'What does he do?' asked Anna, hoping to shift to safer ground. All this was really most surprising and unorthodox.

'At the moment, nothing,' said Joan and her beautiful dark eyes clouded. 'He can't stick at anything. He's had twelve jobs in the last four years and now he's just had the sack from the travel agency. That's why he's here. He's broke.'

'But surely,' Anna expostulated, 'he can find *something* to do. He can't like sponging on you!'

Joan drew a long, luxurious breath through her black cigarette holder.

'Anna, my child, I love you dearly but I must shock your innocent heart by telling you frankly that "sponging on me", as you call it, is exactly what Maurice *does* like doing.'

'But no decent man – ' began Anna indignantly.

'There are men and men,' said Joan equably. 'Those that you have met are doubtless good honest God-fearing types in the backwoods of Essex who fairly relish a hard day's toil. But believe you me, they're not all like that. Maurice, for one, loathes any effort. You saw his keenness to put in an hour's mild sweating at the Youth Club tonight.'

'But he may stay on indefinitely,' faltered Anna, the foundations of her calm ordered world rolling dangerously. 'And suppose he wants to get married one day?'

'How long he stays,' said Joan, 'depends on how tough I can be with him. I'm much too easy-going I know. And as for marrying, it's the best thing he could do, providing his wife can support him.'

'It all seems so dreadfully *wrong*,' persisted Anna helplessly. 'Why should a girl like you be battened on by a perfectly strong young man who can earn his own living?'

Joan smiled. To Anna she looked suddenly immensely wise and beautiful.

'It isn't really a matter of being a man or a woman, you know. The world has its weaklings in both sexes, you'll find – and Maurice is one of them. He can stay here until I really am broke myself. Then, I suspect, he'll find some other soft-headed host to be a parasite upon.'

She spoke entirely without rancour, her manner as gay and debonair as ever. Suddenly she leapt to her feet.

'But that's enough of Maurice. Let's bring the food in here and have it on our laps!'

The rest of the evening passed more lightly. They discussed the chances of Miss Enderby in what Andy Craig ribaldly called 'The New School Stakes', they talked of books and the theatre, and Anna was shown Joan Berry's extensive wardrobe which filled her with envy and delight. She tried on hats and jewellery, attempted to press her broad country feet into Joan's elegant shoes, with no success, and submitted herself to a face massage with a new expensive lotion teeming with hormones, vitamins, and moisturizers.

They played the gramophone, and listened to the radio, and Maurice's name was not mentioned again until Anna was putting on her coat and shivering already with the thought of facing the bitter night outside.

She caught sight again of the gaudy travel pamphlets which winked from the floor.

'You didn't say where you'd decided to go, you know,' she said to Joan, as she pulled on her gloves.

'I shall probably spend my summer holiday right here,' said Joan lightly. 'Don't forget I have Maurice still in my hair, and despite the economists I don't find that two can live as cheaply as one!'

As she waited for her bus in the wind-swept street Anna had food for thought. How little one knew of people! And how much finer they were when one knew more about them! She thought guiltily of her airy dismissal of Joan as a vain flibber-tigibbet, of Andy Craig as a worthless show-off, of Alan Foster as a spineless windbag.

A stray cat, thin but sociable, appeared from an alley and weaved its bony length sensuously about her legs.

'Maybe I don't know much after all,' said Anna to the cat as she bent to fondle its bitten ears. 'There's one thing I've learnt tonight. Joan Berry's a greater person than ever I can hope to be!'

12. Miss Enderby Takes Up Arms

JOAN BERRY'S revelations caused Anna to look upon her colleagues with fresh understanding. The thought that Tom Drew, for instance, left the snug haven of Mrs Armstrong's house to help with boxing sessions at the Youth Club on wintry nights made her like that young man even more.

An incident occurred, too, that same week which showed Miss Enderby in a decidedly more favourable light.

One morning Anna was hearing six of her slowest children read. This was a task which she had to drive herself to do, so formidable and torturing was it. The blank bewilderment on the children's faces as they confronted their simple pages, the peculiar and unintelligible sounds which they gave forth, bearing no relation to the words before them, and their complete inability to remember Anna's kindly explanations were enough to daunt the stoutest heart.

Beyond the little circle at her desk, the rest of the class had divided itself into half a dozen groups and read noisily under the vociferous charge of their reading leaders. In the midst of this infernal bedlam, accompanied by the confusion of building noises outside, the door opened and Miss Enderby beckoned Anna mysteriously to her side.

'Can you leave them for a moment, dear?' she asked, her gaze on Arnold who, oblivious of the eye of authority, was about to hit his neighbour a satisfying wallop over the head with his *Happy Valley Reader*.

'It might be as well to leave someone in charge,' said Anna hastily, and clapped her hands thunderously.

'I'm looking for a sensible child to take charge,' announced Anna, above the hum which had succeeded the uproar. As if by magic, silence fell. Arms were folded, tongues stilled, faces became angelic and demure, and feet were placed decorously side by side. Anna, luxuriating in the sudden unaccustomed peace, let her glance wander over this band of meek cherubs.

'I think,' she said slowly, at last, 'it should be Angela.'

At once the silence was broken by the susurration of released breath and the relaxation of bodies, while Angela, a fat young lady with pigtails, bustled importantly to the front of the class.

'Them girls!' said someone in a disgruntled aside. 'Always them girls!'

'Just get on with your reading,' said Miss Enderby majestically, 'and Angela can tell Miss Lacey who has worked well when she returns.'

She bent sideways to Anna and said softly: 'The *positive* approach is always best.'

'Of course,' said Anna politely. Miss Enderby's figure stiffened, even as she spoke. Her eye had again alighted upon Arnold who was now bending back the covers of his *Happy Valley Reader* with such energy that reports like pistol shots were flying from the protesting volume.

'Of course,' said Miss Enderby, raising her voice, 'Angela is quite at liberty to report *bad behaviour* to Miss Lacey. And I shall be waiting in my room for any child who disgraces himself!'

Arnold replaced his book meekly on the desk. Miss Enderby, with a final stern glance, sailed into the corridor followed by Anna who wondered if Miss Enderby's last admonition could be called 'the negative approach' to good conduct.

It was blissfully quiet in the corridor. Miss Enderby stopped, not far from Anna's room and faced her youngest member of staff. Her expression was unusually grave and Anna began to feel very uncomfortable. What could she have done? She began to rack her conscience for sins committed and omitted, and though a host of them rose at once, like so many black rooks, not one seemed to warrant the solemnity of her headmistress's demeanour.

'Now,' said Miss Enderby, looking up and down the empty corridor. 'I want you to tell me the truth, my dear.'

'Naturally,' said Anna shortly, panic flooding her. What on earth had she done? Could that light tap on the side of Betty Fellows's head last week have occasioned acute meningitis? Had that half aspirin, administered to Johnny Bates yesterday, caused his death during the night? Both children were now away from school.

Miss Enderby enlightened her before Anna could think of further unnerving possibilities.

'I have had a most serious accusation made against you by Mrs Bond.'

'Mrs Bond!' echoed Anna blankly. Janet Bond was an inoffensive little mouse of a child, with wispy fair hair and a pointed pink nose. As far as Anna could remember she had never had cause to speak an angry word to the child.

'Mrs Bond,' went on Miss Enderby solemnly, 'tells me that you swore at her daughter yesterday afternoon.'

'Swore?' squeaked Anna indignantly. 'I don't swear. At least, not in school,' she added honestly. 'But never, never at Janet Bond. There's never been any need. *Arnold* now – ' Her voice trailed away.

'Mrs Bond's story is that Janet was a little late back to school in the afternoon. According to her the child was obliged to spend some time in the lavatory – some nonsense about a dose of medicine, which I don't agree with – but it meant she set out a little late.'

'Just a minute,' said Anna, light breaking. 'She did come late, *very* late. I'd closed the register and marked her absent, of course. Then she wandered in, when we'd started our paper-cutting and I believe I said she was a nuisance. She didn't appear to hear, and was certainly quite unmoved and cheerful.'

'Ah, a nuisance!' pounced Miss Enderby. 'You're sure you only said "A nuisance"?'

'I may not even have said that,' protested Anna. 'It was no more than a faint irritation that I felt – and I certainly didn't swear!'

'Mrs Bond maintains that you called her child "A blasted nuisance". Is that true?'

'Indeed it isn't,' said Anna·stoutly. 'The child – or the mother – has made it up!'

Miss Enderby's face relaxed and she patted Anna's shoulder.

'As I suspected, my dear, but of course I had to make sure.' She braced her fine shoulders, her eyes sparkling.

'Follow me, dear,' she said. 'Mrs Bond's in my room and I'd like you to meet her.'

She swept, with stately tread, down the long corridor. Anna, her fears returning, although her conscience, on this score at least, was clear, wondered just what sort of monster would confront her in Miss Enderby's room. She had heard of irate parents. Now, alas, she was to meet one face to face!

Anna's overstrung imagination had envisaged an Amazon of at least six feet in height of militant aspect and powerful physique. Something red-faced, with flashing eyes, possibly brandishing a weapon, and almost certainly wearing a man's cloth cap and formidable boots was the object upon which Anna feared that she must look. It was, therefore, with a shock of relief that she first saw Mrs Bond.

She was as mouse-like as her daughter, with fair, pretty, faded good looks. A missing tooth gave an added childishness to her meek appearance as she smiled deprecatingly at Miss Enderby.

Her headmistress, Anna noticed, was now buoyantly in command. She sailed into action with considerable dash.

'This is Miss Lacey, Mrs Bond, Janet's teacher.'

'Pleased to meet you, miss,' said Mrs Bond nervously. Anna

suspected that any fight which Mrs Bond had had on arrival at
Miss Enderby's room had gradually run out of her heels whilst
she had been left kicking them in that lady's sanctum. Could
Miss Enderby have meant that to happen, Anna wondered?
She must know all the strategies of parent–teacher warfare.
Anna began to feel a little braver.

Miss Enderby settled herself briskly at her desk, pulled
forward a clean sheet of paper and, pen poised, leant graciously
towards Mrs Bond.

'Now, Mrs Bond,' she began firmly, 'in Miss Lacey's presence, would you be kind enough to repeat your allegation?'

'Repeat what?' asked Mrs Bond, eyes widening.

'Repeat your statement. Tell me again about Miss Lacey's
bad language to your child in front of the class.'

Mrs Bond looked confused.

'Well, I don't hardly like –' she began uncomfortably. Miss
Enderby's pen rapped peremptorily on the desk.

'Mrs Bond, will you please repeat your statement? Then
I shall ask you to sign it while I ring the police and explain
things.'

'The *police*?' yelped Mrs Bond, rising smartly from her seat.
'What's the police got to do with it?'

'You surely understand,' said Miss Enderby, raising her fine
eyebrows, 'that you cannot come here and make allegations
of such a serious nature against one of my staff without putting
the whole affair into the hands of the justices. Miss Lacey, one
of my most trusted members of staff, is at the beginning of a
distinguished career, we all believe. If your allegation is found
to be true it will seriously jeopardize her hopes later. Her good
name will be damaged. I must see it cleared.'

Anna stood, marvelling at such brave tactics. Mrs Bond,
looking distinctly shattered, gazed from one to the other.

'I'm not getting mixed up with no police,' she said obstin-
ately. 'Perhaps Miss Lacey here can tell me what really happened. Children do make up things sometimes.'

'You should have thought of that before,' pointed out Miss Enderby. 'I really think you have been too hasty. I am quite willing – and so of course is Miss Lacey – to let the case come to court. We can't have accusations being made against the staff. It gives Elm Hill School a bad name. Miss Lacey, explain once more, would you, dear?'

She lay back in her armchair, eyes closed, with the tips of her beringed fingers placed judicially together, and listened to Anna's faltering account of the incident.

'Oh well,' said Mrs Bond, 'that's all right then. I see it all now. Been a mistake – that's all. You know what kids are – like to exaggerate any little thing.'

Miss Enderby sat up with a jerk.

'Mrs Bond,' she said with slow emphasis, 'this is not "a little thing". Are you satisfied with Miss Lacey's explanation?'

'Oh yes,' breathed Mrs Bond earnestly.

'And you agree that Janet has not told the truth in this matter?'

'Oh, I do, I do,' said Mrs Bond, bridling self-righteously, 'and when her dad hears about this he won't half give her what for!'

'Oh *please* –' began Anna pleadingly, horrified at any violence being done to her diminutive, if untruthful, pupil.

'You must do as you think fit,' said Miss Enderby ponderously, with a quelling sidelong glance at Anna who was struck silent. 'But if I were in your position I should say nothing of this – er – regrettable episode to my husband. You have behaved rather foolishly, you know. A quiet word to Janet should be enough to stop any further tale-bearing, and I really think that it's a case of "Least said, soonest mended".'

'Oh yes, miss: I'm sure you're right, miss,' agreed Mrs Bond hastily. 'I'm sorry I've caused such a lot of trouble. I really am.'

Miss Enderby permitted a small sad smile to curve her lips. She sighed gently and wearily.

'We're quite used to trouble, Mrs Bond. All teachers are – but we always hope for cooperation from our parents to help lighten the task. It is a great grief to us when we find ourselves attacked by those we had imagined to be our friends.'

She really is superb! thought Anna. After the running through, the sad wiping of the sword blade, with one foot still upon the victim – it was masterly! But genuine gratitude too overwhelmed young Anna. She had been most gallantly defended from her enemy and she felt a new warmth towards her headmistress.

'So, I take it, you *completely withdraw* your remarks about Miss Lacey?' pressed Miss Enderby, rising behind her desk to show that the interview had reached its end.

'Oh yes indeed,' gabbled Mrs Bond, her eyes moist with emotion. 'I won't say nothing more – not even to Harold! You've both been ever so nice about it. I can see I was a bit wrought-up like.'

Miss Enderby inclined her head graciously.

'Then we'll tear this up and forget it,' she said, raising the blank sheet of paper as though it were covered in the vilest accusations. She tore it ceremoniously across and tossed it, with superb accuracy, into the waste-paper basket.

'There!' said Miss Enderby, coming across the carpet and clasping Mrs Bond's hand, more in sorrow than in anger. 'And in future, Mrs Bond, remember that we are as devoted to your child as you are yourself, and please, I beg of you, try to *trust* us!'

There was a moving tremolo in the last sentence which caused a lurking tear to burst from Mrs Bond's eye and trickle down her mouse-like pink nose as she made her way into the corridor.

Anna waited by the desk until Miss Enderby returned from showing her visitor out. The headmistress's face glowed with righteous victory.

'It's always best to be *absolutely firm*,' she announced briskly.

'Now, child, back to your class. They've been left long enough.'

'Miss Enderby,' Anna burst out, 'thank you enormously. You were absolutely wonderful!'

'Oh tush, child,' said Miss Enderby chidingly, but she looked pleased at Anna's outburst, and admired the sapphire on her hand rather self-consciously. 'I only did what any head teacher would do – backed up my staff and my school. Can't have Elm Hill's name dragged in the mud – particularly just now.'

'Of course not,' said Anna, cooling slightly. Had her headmistress, after all, only been defending her own, with no real feeling for Anna as a person? Miss Enderby had looked up and was watching her closely.

'You *didn't* swear, I suppose?' she asked softly.

'No, I didn't!' said Anna, so indignantly that it was almost a shout. 'I thought you believed me!'

'I did, my dear,' said Miss Enderby calmly. 'I still do – but I always like to be *quite sure*. Now run along and see to your class.'

Anna, much shaken by all that had happened, returned slowly to the classroom, glad of the quiet corridor's length which gave her time to compose herself.

Yes, Florence Enderby was magnificent, thought Anna, and her admiration for her had increased threefold. But still through all the storm, her headmistress had clung to her own ambition. Nothing should tarnish the name of Elm Hill – for Elm Hill was synonymous with Florence Enderby, the candidate for the new school which was now growing so rapidly beside it. By the time Anna reached her own door she faced the fact, yet again, that she was learning, not only her job, but a mighty lot about human nature at Elm Hill.

To her amazement her classroom was tranquil under the eagle eye of Angela who had ensconced herself in Anna's seat.

Anna felt a sudden rush of affection for her motley crowd of children, born of relief from tension and the return to normal working conditions. Here she was safe, here was a job to do, here she was liked and her word – if not exactly law – was, occasionally, listened to. For the first time in her teaching career Anna felt sure of herself. Could it be the knowledge that she had Miss Enderby's support behind her that gave her this blessed warmth of spirit?

Whatever it was it should be acknowledged, thought Anna happily.

'Get out the sweet tin,' she commanded the beaming Angela. 'And give *two* to everybody!'

The rapturous shout which greeted this announcement must have penetrated to Miss Enderby's sanctum, so lustily did it ring out. But Anna, full-hearted, did nothing to quell it.

13. Mrs Flynn's Tea Party

As March broke, the fields of home were brushed with tender green, and Anna rejoiced to see the catkins streaming bravely in the wind and the bright crocuses following hard on the heels of the snowdrops and aconites in the farm garden.

There were young lambs in her father's fields, and two motherless ones in the stable across the yard, which she helped to feed by bottle. They were vociferously hungry, and when the bottle was emptied would suck energetically at Anna's fingers, clamping them firmly between the warm ribbed roofs of their mouths and their rough tongues.

Young Ted fed them more often than anyone and as the weeks passed they grew much attached to him, following him across the yard and greeting him with ecstatic bleatings. He christened them Gilbert and Sullivan, being a devotee of the operas, and maintained stoutly that the two lambs answered to their names.

He had settled in easily and was proving himself a conscientious and intelligent worker. Anna's parents accepted him happily as one of the family, but Anna was not completely at ease in the young man's company.

He had begun to look at her with a certain dog-like devotion that caused her some alarm. His initial shyness had been replaced by a tendency to follow her about the farm rather as Gilbert and Sullivan followed him. He made excuses to stay at the Laceys at weekends, when formerly he went home and Anna's heart dropped on many a Friday evening when she burst into the farmhouse to find Ted's great bulk rising eagerly from an armchair to greet her.

She did not dislike the boy, but she preferred to have her parents' company undiluted at weekends. She realized that her father was only too pleased to have such willing help and that her mother probably thought that Ted's young company was pleasant to her, but in fact she found it irksome.

It could be so dangerously easy for Anna and Ted to slip into an engagement and then marriage. Nothing would appear more suitable. A farmer's daughter marrying a young farmer who would be heir to his father's neighbouring farm, known to each other, and the district, from babyhood – what could be more delightful? It was this very suitability that put Anna on her guard and made her look upon young Ted's lovesick countenance with some dismay.

Life was too full and too exciting to be tied down yet. There was so much to do and so much to learn about matters and people, as Anna was fast discovering. Such a long-term decision as choosing a husband could not possibly be undertaken yet, but Anna knew already, with a wisdom beyond her years, that Ted would never do. Sweet and slow by nature he would accept all that Anna said and did, and think it wonderful. And Anna was quite sure that to be put on a pedestal was neither right nor at all what she wanted.

The vagaries of human nature, about which Anna learnt more daily, were displayed to her fascinated gaze one spring afternoon when Mrs Flynn gave a tea party.

The fact that Mrs Flynn proposed such an extravagant act was almost unbelievable. Anna accepted the invitation to tea in the sitting-room with due solemnity and wondered what there would be to eat and who the other guests might be, in that order. She still had a healthy appetite, only half-satisfied by Mrs Flynn's meagre fare and the school dinners which left much to be desired.

On the great day she let herself in at the front door, as quietly as the obdurate piece of timber would allow, and crept upstairs to put on a fresh frock. The sound of voices raised in ladylike conversation filtered through the sitting-room door, while the largest kettle in the kitchen filled that tiny room with steam.

On entering the sitting-room she was first staggered by Mrs Flynn's unwonted smartness. She was arrayed in a checked worsted suit which Anna had never seen before. That it should be new was of course too much to hope from one of Mrs Flynn's calibre, and the fact that it had been preserved for many years was apparent from the well-padded shoulders and small lapels which dated from the military influence of the last war. There emanated too from it a faint but unmistakable smell of mothballs, and the velvet collar showed a central crease born of long folding. The blouse which she wore under it was a frothy affair of pink lace, adorned with a sparkling paste bow with only one stone missing. Anna suspected, rightly enough, that it was really a 'dicky' with a net back and elastic round the bottom, and secretly hoped that Mrs Flynn might take off her jacket in a moment of mental aberration so that she might see if she were right; though even as this delicious and irreverent thought flitted through her mind Anna realized sadly that Mrs Flynn would never forget herself to such an extent.

There were two guests, seated rather uncomfortably on Mrs Flynn's painfully 'contemporary' couch. One was a vast woman in a ruched velvet pancake of a hat, who was introduced as Mrs Porter, and the other a small dark woman, with such a large hairy mole on her chin that Anna had great difficulty in averting her gaze from it. She, Mrs Flynn explained, was Mrs Adams whose husband worked in the Council Offices.

From the way Mrs Flynn's voice took on a respectful note whilst imparting this last piece of information Anna gathered two things – firstly, that Mrs Porter had no husband, and secondly that it was Mrs Adams's husband's eminent position which gave her the status which so impressed Mrs Flynn.

They were an easy pair to entertain for Anna soon found

that they much preferred talking to listening and she was very content, after a day's work, to sit back and nod and smile whilst the ladies chattered on.

An unusually hot fire warmed the sitting-room. Anna could see that the key of the gas fire was almost perpendicular which meant that it was almost fully on. Such bounty could only mean that Mrs Flynn desired to impress. The tea-table too was packed with iced buns, horribly dainty tomato sandwiches, brown bread and butter, white bread and butter, two kinds of jam, some rather nasty fish-paste, and a dish of rich fruit cake cut into cubes so minute that one might have called it diced, thought Anna, as she accepted an oblong crumb with every appearance of delight. However, this was rich fare compared with her usual Osborne-biscuits-and-weak-tea meal and she made the most of the occasion by eating as heartily as politeness and Mrs Flynn's cautious passing would allow.

Conversation turned to the vicar of the parish, led that way by Mrs Porter who was obviously a supporter of the church. How useful vicars are, thought Anna remembering other tea-parties, running as they do a close second to the weather as a conversational topic!

'He takes the service so *beautifully*,' confided Mrs Porter, her well-powdered jowls wobbling with the intensity of her utterances. 'So reverently! And of course, his voice is quite *wonderful*!'

'Really?' said Mrs Flynn, trying to appear suitably impressed and look in her guests' cups at the same time.

'My husband always said a good voice was the most important asset of a clergyman. My husband was in *oil*,' she added turning to Anna.

Anna fought down an insane desire to ask 'Boiling?' and nodded instead.

'Of course, there are a lot of people,' went on Mrs Porter, 'who *criticize* him. They say that he is too fond of *ritual* and he overdoes the incense and the genuflexions, but personally,

I like it. After all, if one *doesn't*, one can always go to chapel.'

'I go to chapel,' said Mrs Adams, dangerously calm.

'Well, there you are!' said Mrs Porter, in a faintly patronizing tone. Anna was instantly aware that Mrs Porter had known this all along, and watched the scene with quickened appreciation. Here was self-aggrandizement in action again.

'And you probably enjoy it very much,' continued Mrs Porter indulgently, nodding the ruched pancake. She spoke, thought Anna, as though religion were a comfortable cup of tea, Indian or China, chosen to taste.

'Naturally,' said Mrs. Adams, turning a dusky pink. She took a deep breath as though about to defend her religious principles, but Mrs Flynn, with commendable aplomb, proffered the tomato sandwiches and spoke hastily.

'And your little boy, Mrs Adams? Is he well?'

Mrs Adams's breath expired peacefully through smiling lips.

'Very well indeed. He's the liveliest of the three. I really don't know what we'd do without him now the others are away at school.'

'Such a handsome child,' enthused Mrs Flynn, 'and devoted to you. His little face fairly lights up when he sees you.'

Mrs Adams simpered and looked gratified.

'Well, I must say he almost hero-worships me. It's "Mum this" and "Mum that". I can't do any wrong in that child's eyes.'

Anna, yet again, marvelled at the diversity of opinion on children. Beauty was certainly in the eye of the beholder. She had yet to find any child with the faintest desire to make a hero of herself but this was not the first mother she had heard claiming devoted allegiance so calmly.

'Frankly,' went on Mrs Adams, her voice getting stronger, 'I don't know how people manage *without* children. It seems so unnatural. I suppose they turn to other things for a substitute. Religion, for instance.' She gave a swift sidelong glance at Mrs

Porter who, affecting complete indifference, was studying the tea-leaves at the bottom of her cup.

One all, thought Anna privately. It was Mrs Flynn who saved the situation from becoming ugly.

'It's been a great grief to us that we've never been blessed with a family,' she said, in suitably modulated tones, 'but we can't all be as lucky as you, Mrs Adams.'

Mrs Adams looked uncomfortable. It was a nasty shock to her to realize that in her anxiety to deliver a stunning blow to Mrs Porter she had inadvertently taken a side-swipe at her hostess. Anna could see, from her discomfiture, that she was wondering whether to apologize or ignore the whole concern. Mrs Porter, meanwhile, had brightened considerably at her fellow-guest's *faux pas*.

'Has Lady Parr called on you yet with tickets for the Charity Ball?' she inquired, with fresh zest, of Mrs Flynn.

'No, indeed,' said Mrs Flynn, somewhat taken aback. There was very little calling of any sort done in the muddy new roads of Elm Hill and this was the first she had heard of Lady Parr.

'Doubtless *you* will be there,' continued Mrs Porter turning her soft powdered countenance, like some mammoth marshmallow, towards Mrs Adams. 'It is to take place at the Town Hall where your husband works.'

'We don't go out in the evenings,' said Mrs Adams swiftly. 'We've the child to consider and I wouldn't dream of leaving him with a baby-sitter.'

'So devoted,' breathed Mrs Porter, 'but you really should get out occasionally. All work and no play, you know!' She gave a gay little laugh and a teaspoon slid down the steep incline of her thighs to the floor. Anna bent to retrieve it whilst the barbs flew to and fro above her head.

'I shall get Lady Parr to call specially,' continued Mrs Porter. 'She'll do anything for me – the *dearest* thing, though a little eccentric. Personally I don't mind her decorating her hats with fresh flowers, even if they *are* ox-eyed daisies; in fact, I think it shows breeding to be above petty formalities. Some people are so small-minded. I suppose it's all a matter of upbringing.'

'Oh, please don't bother her,' said Mrs Adams off-handedly. 'We live so modestly – well within our income I'm glad to say, we've both a horror of debt – that I doubt if Lady Parr would want to visit us. In your case it's quite different, of course. You have such a beautiful house and garden, it must be a pleasure for you to entertain.'

Anna was suddenly reminded of a short story that she had once read, called *The Octave of Jealousy* by Stacey Aumonier. It began with the meeting of a tramp with a labourer whom he envied. The labourer in turn envied a slightly more prosperous gamekeeper, the gamekeeper envied the neighbouring shop-keeper, and so on until the tale came full circle, and the great man, bowed down with responsibilities, looked at the carefree tramp and envied his freedom from the bottom of his heart. Here, before her, was Mrs Flynn envying the slightly exalted status of Mrs Adams whose husband was a Council official. Mrs Adams, in turn, envied Mrs Porter's more spacious house and garden and, one suspected from her remarks about her own devotion to her children, Mrs Porter's freedom from family cares. Mrs Porter, it appeared, aspired to be Lady Parr's confidante and equal. Really, thought Anna, the whole thing would be amusing if it were not so pathetic and so soul-destroying to the status-seekers.

It was with relief that she saw Mrs Porter heave herself at last from the couch to make her farewells. Mrs Adams left at the same time. Anna watched them part at the gate with much cordiality and thought what a wonderful thing civilization was.

Mrs Flynn came hurrying back flushed with the success of her tea-party.

'Well, I hope they enjoyed themselves,' said Mrs Flynn. 'They're two nice women, with a lot in common.'

And that's true enough, Anna thought. Fighters both, with eyes alert for a stranglehold! But aloud she said:

'It was a wonderful tea, Mrs Flynn,' and helped her pack the debris of this miraculous meal on to a tray.

Mrs Flynn smiled graciously at the compliment, but, even as she smiled, she bent to turn out the gas fire.

The invitation to tea at Tom Drew's had been repeated several times, and now that the evenings were getting lighter and the hint of spring could be felt even in the desert wastes of Elm Hill, they had taken to walking the few sad footpaths that still threaded the neighbourhood.

One of their favourite walks was along the tow-path of a canal. The tranquil water mirrored the raggle-taggle trees and scruffy banks, both scarred by urchins' play, and cast up a green and kindly reflection. The noise of traffic from the roads near by was always with them, and the factory hooters sent the singing blackbirds squawking in fright across their path, but it was the nearest that this country-starved couple could find to their natural background, and their pleasure in each other's company mitigated the wretched mess of their surroundings.

Anna told Tom about Mrs Flynn's famous tea-party, with a wealth of mirthful detail which amused him.

'But it's really terribly sad,' said Anna, suddenly serious. 'I mean, those poor women – making themselves so miserable, wanting things so badly! Things that really don't matter a button!'

'That's what's wrong with nine-tenths of the people you meet,' asserted Tom, with the downrightness of youth.

'As far as I can see they don't interest themselves in making things. They don't enjoy looking at plants or trees or lovely buildings –'

'Not much scope here,' pointed out Anna reasonably.

'Maybe not, but there's no need to turn exclusively to the

TV and your neighbours' good luck for your interests. What beats me,' went on Tom warmly, 'is the neglect of simple pleasures and the complete loss of – well – wonder. Why, I get a thrill every time I plant something that looks like a dead flea and up comes a great, glorious, pulsing flower! Who wouldn't?'

'You've got the knack of happy living,' commented Anna. 'I think you must be like my mother who says that you aren't just given happiness. She says you have to pick it up here and there all through the day. And she does too. She smells a rose, or she marvels at a bird hanging upside down on a spray, she makes a perfect dinner. She really savours life, you know, and from it she builds up a stock of happiness.'

'She sounds as though she's discovered the secret,' said Tom. 'Have you?'

Their footsteps had slowed and they now stood by the canal. Anna bent to pick up a pebble and tossed it into the quiet water, shattering the mirrored picture into a million dancing pieces.

'Not as well,' replied Anna slowly. 'She has so many more interests, now I come to think of it. She reads a lot of poetry, for one thing.'

'She sounds quite a poet herself,' said Tom. 'She can find the essence of things.'

'And, of course, now I'm teaching there doesn't seem to be much time,' continued Anna, still perplexed. She turned to look at Tom with troubled blue eyes.

Tom laughed happily and chucked her under the chin kindly.

'Cheer up, you'll do! But take my warning. Don't you start being a specialist, young Anna, it cramps one's pleasures. So many things, as your mother says, can make happiness and thank God there are still plenty of them.'

He turned Anna round and they started to return.

'Let's run,' said Tom, 'it's getting cold. We'll hare back and light a fire. Now, there's a pleasure for you – a real elemental one. And there's a bottle of wine on the shelf!'

In great good spirits they jog-trotted along the rough tow-path while the water beside them changed from green to black and the headlights on the busy highway pricked the twilight with stabbing gleaming needles.

PART THREE

New Growth

14. Classroom Troubles

As the end of her second term loomed in sight Anna began to feel more used to school life, though there were still some aspects of it which she found disconcerting.

She had not reckoned, for one thing, on the constant interruptions that would crop up during a lesson. The incidental class interruptions she soon became used to, the requests for drinks of water, trips to the lavatory, and forgotten handkerchiefs left in coat pockets. Many, she suspected, were concocted – any excuse to break the monotony of class routine – and her ignorance was being exploited by these astute young barbarians, and as she grew more experienced she squashed these classroom interruptions ruthlessly.

But interruptions from outside were incessant. Besides the constant background of building noises, there seemed to be an unending flow of children entering the classroom with some message or other demanding urgent attention, or bearing lost property.

One morning Anna had dealt with a raincoat belt which had been found and was brought in proudly by a smug infant only too pleased to be missing a Scripture lesson whilst touring the school, a scarf found in the playground, three handkerchiefs, and two notes from other teachers.

The story of Daniel in the lions' den progressed in spasmodic jerks as the door opened and shut, time and time again. The interludes followed a set pattern. The entering child planted itself before the class, held up the object needing an owner, and said importantly:

'Anyone's here?'

A full-throated chorus of:

'No! Not 'ere, mate! 'Tain't ours!' would blast the invader, who would smirk at Anna and retire to continue the pleasurable progress.

At last Anna determined to take a stand. She would finish the story of Daniel despite interruptions. She posted Janet, the militant Mrs Bond's daughter, at the door and forbade her to let anyone enter. As she did not want the child to miss the story, nor did she want Miss Enderby to see a child of hers waiting outside the door as though banished for bad behaviour she let Janet stay inside, with one hand on the door knob.

'And when I can see faces and not backs of heads, and when you've quite finished talking, David Watts, and you've finished tying up your shoe-laces, Jean Pratt – then I'll go on with the story,' said Anna tartly.

Gradually the turmoil subsided and in the fitful peace which followed, she continued.

' So Darius realized that he had been tricked by the presidents and princes, and he felt very sorry for Daniel who had been thrown to the lions –'

There was a scuffling at the door. It opened a crack and was promptly slammed back by Janet. The heads which, on the whole, had been turned towards Anna, now swivelled doorwards.

'He felt very ashamed of himself,' continued Anna doggedly, 'and spent the night praying. He could not sleep –'

A sustained thumping began at the door and some of the class began to snigger and exchange delighted glances.

'Nor could he eat, Arnold,' said Anna, glaring at the malefactor. 'And as soon as morning broke he –'

A piping sound was added to the thumping, and the door began to edge open. Janet, pressing against it with her shoulder, began to break into giggling protests.

'Can't help it, miss. He keeps all on pushing, miss. It's a infant, miss.'

'Let him in,' said Anna savagely.

Janet swung back the door to reveal a two-foot high cherub

holding a brown paper carrier bag with great care. His face was wreathed in triumphant smiles at having at last gained access.

'Stand by the cupboard till I've finished,' snapped Anna. The smiles vanished and a woebegone expression, which normally would have melted Anna's kind heart, replaced it. Bewildered but obedient he took his place, occasionally peering into the depths of the bag.

The children watched him with interest and though Anna continued with the tale of Daniel's vindication with all the narrating powers she could muster, yet she was conscious of having lost the major part of their attention.

'And so,' she wound up, 'Darius wrote the decree saying that Daniel's God was the true one, and Daniel was recognized as a very brave and honest man.'

She turned impatiently to the waiting figure.

'Let's see. Quickly now,' she said imperiously, as the child started towards her. And what might that contain this time? Anna wondered. Half-a-dozen gym shoes, all odd? A derelict train set? A couple of jigsaw puzzles, hopelessly muddled together? Anna was fast becoming acquainted with the flotsam and jetsam thrown up by the surging waves of school life.

The child, beaming again, parted the top of the bag carefully.

'Would you like to show your class –' he began, as though repeating a lesson.

'Yes, yes!' said Anna hastily, thrusting her hand into the depths. She withdrew it rapidly, with a yelp.

The bag contained a fine hedgehog.

*

School dinners, too, were another occupational hazard, Anna soon discovered. The noise and the children's appalling table manners almost overwhelmed her, and she certainly had very little appetite for the food which she was obliged to eat in their company.

Their home backgrounds varied, she knew, and she was prepared for a certain amount of slovenly behaviour. But almost all ate with their mouths open, displaying half-masticated food in the most nauseating way, and they crammed in great spoonfuls far beyond the comfortable capacity of their mouths. This was partly greed, she realized, and partly excitement; but she noticed in her classroom, as well as in the dining-room, that a large proportion of the children breathed through their mouths rather than their noses. When she tried to correct this she discovered that almost all the children found nasal breathing difficult, and could only suppose that this was due to a variety of reasons – possibly adenoids, possibly habitual catarrh, due in some cases, she suspected, to a diet almost exclusively of starch, and, of course, to wrong breathing habits started in babyhood and now firmly established. In any case, this common malady did nothing to help their mode of eating and even Anna's robust appetite failed her at midday dinner.

The children were allowed to talk, but their voices, raised above the clatter of their knives and forks, the crashing of plates and each other's conversation, soon reached such a crescendo of noise that the teacher in charge would ring a bell and demand silence, every now and again. Added to this the food was so badly cooked and served that it was a wonder to Anna that the children attacked it with such gusto.

Their favourite sweet was red jelly with blobs of *ersatz* cream tasting and smelling like face cream. This was greeted with roars of applause when it appeared at the serving hatch, and the long line of children bearing their plates progressed at a smarter pace than usual as each child hoped to polish off his first plateful in the expectation of a second helping. And many a grubby finger was run unhygienically round the plate and sucked loudly and lovingly to savour the last morsels of this delectable sweet.

Another problem, which Anna found a difficult one to solve, was the management of her classwork as opposed to everyday teaching and discipline.

Preparing lessons was a fairly straightforward business, undertaken in the evenings, in the comparative peace of Mrs Flynn's establishment, and with the help of reference books, maps, pictures, and so on. Catching and holding her class's attention was becoming easier as the months passed and Anna's authority was recognized by the children and her own self-confidence grew. But there were difficulties in organizing the children's work which Anna had heard nothing of at college.

Apart from the impossibly large number in the classroom which was the arch-problem, there was the difference in speed at which children worked. Poor Anna found that she would spend most of her precious dinner hour in putting out paper and crayons for an afternoon's art lesson, would spend ten minutes or more explaining carefully that they were going to attempt to design an all-over wallpaper pattern, would show them how to fold their paper and perhaps give a few simple examples to start the more adenoidal and inartistic members of the class, and would then relax in the hope that the rest of the lesson, stretching ahead for another forty minutes, would be happily and usefully filled with artistic endeavour.

Alas for such fond hopes! Within five minutes two or three slapdash individuals would have scrawled a motif in each square, coloured it in with a frantic crayon and rushed to Anna for approval.

'Finished!' they would say proudly, sniffing cheerfully. 'Can we draw on the back?'

At first Anna would protest. The pattern was too sketchy, it was carelessly done, they must go back and improve it. And they were not to hurry. There would be no prizes, Anna said firmly, for the people who finished first.

Sometimes this worked, but with the one or two incorrigibly lazy it became simpler to let them turn over and expend what little energy and talent they had in drawing cowboys and Indians, ponies, ballet dancers, or simply a mammoth Union Jack in variegated colours – this last a firm favourite with the really backward members of the class.

At the other extreme, of course, would be the painstaking perfectionists who rubbed out as fast as they drew, and attempted designs of such intricacy and flamboyancy that only half the work was completed when the bell rang for playtime. Then there would be a great outcry for more time to finish.

'Can't we do them after play?'

'Can't we crayon while you read us *The Heroes*?'

'Can we take them home to finish them?'

'Oh, Miss! Please, miss! Oh, miss, do let's!'

It was a basic problem of class management which could only be mitigated, and never completely overcome.

Anna's severest shock, in this connexion, came one day when she decided to look through her class's work-books. Each child had one of three large paper-covered books containing English exercises, lists of spellings, general knowledge, diagrams, and pictures. The work was largely self-corrective and the advantage of the scheme was the fact that each child could work steadily at its own pace.

'Their work-books,' Miss Enderby had said casually to Anna, 'need not be taken in for correction very often. Their ordinary exercise books for arithmetic, English, nature, history, and so on, must be carefully corrected after each piece of work, and the corrections checked too.'

Anna had felt thankful that at least one of the books in each of the forty-eight desks could be left to look after itself for a week or two, and she was only too delighted to see the children busily working away, at odd times, in these books which they much enjoyed using.

The results, she found, on looking them through were disastrous. There seemed to have been a great competition going on to see how many pages could be filled up in the shortest time. Scrawls, illegible scribbles, and sometimes hasty dashes where the answer was not even attempted disfigured the pages and – worse still – the work-books designed to give useful instruction for about a term, were filled in a matter of a fortnight. What would the ratepayers think, Anna wondered, appalled, as she looked at this wantonness?

These difficulties she overcame to some extent by using odd sheets of paper made into simple one-section books one hand-work lesson by her class. These they called their 'Busy books', and when the covers had been thus lovingly inscribed, and then decorated, they were encouraged to spend the odd minutes, in which they might be waiting, in writing down useful lists, copying in short poems which they liked, items of news, or simply drawing pictures. It gave an outlet to their inventiveness and the more expensive work-books resumed their proper function.

All this took time to learn. It was experience bitterly bought, Anna found, at the cost of her own nervous energy and anxiety. Would any of these difficulties matter so much with a class of half the size, she sometimes wondered? Did Miss Anderson, at the village school at home, face quite such problems? In comparison, Anna thought, remembering her visit just after Christmas, it seemed like the land of the lotus-eaters.

An incident occurred one day which made Anna realize that size of class was indeed only comparative. Miss Enderby had opened her door one morning and in had filed a dozen or so beaming children, each clutching a chair, a pencil, several books, and other odds and ends.

'Do you mind having a few extra for today, dear?' asked Miss Enderby. Anna felt rightly that this question needed no answer and tried to look welcoming. It was at times like this that she thought enviously of the old-fashioned double desks in the village school where two small bodies could slide obligingly to one end of the bench to make room for a third without the encumbrance of extra chairs in the classroom.

The newcomers ranged themselves as neatly as they could in the little space available and held excited conversations with their friends in Anna's class who welcomed this diversion from normal routine.

'It's Mr Drew's class, dear,' said Miss Enderby. 'I'm having to divide them between four of you as I've a committee meeting at the Town Hall unfortunately. Otherwise, of course, I could take them myself.'

'Is he ill?' asked Anna in surprise. She had spent the evening before with him and he had seemed in his usual robust health then.

'His father has been taken ill. A telegram arrived this morning. A stroke, I gather, poor fellow. Mr Drew has gone straight off. It's most worrying for him.'

Poor Tom, thought Anna, it certainly would be a shock. She only hoped that things would not be as bad when he arrived as he would be imagining them on his long journey.

But her sympathy for Tom had to be put aside under the pressure of immediate circumstances. To keep over sixty children happily occupied in a confined space is not easy, especially when there are not enough desks to allow pencils and papers to be used.

They read, but those with no desks had their books at uncomfortable angles and soon fell to fidgeting. They sang, they took it in turns to recite poems and to tell stories. Anna read fairy tales to them until her throat ached. At last she could bear the oppressive mass of children no longer and, throwing the timetable to the winds she escorted her mammoth class into the playground.

It was wonderful to feel the wind on her face after the stuffy classroom. The children were unwontedly excited and rushed madly about, obeying the blasts of Anna's whistle far from promptly. How much more difficult it was to manage sixty-odd than forty-eight, thought poor Anna.

She tipped up the box of balls which she had brought out with her and the children ran hither and thither to grab one apiece. At length Anna shrilled her whistle.

'Hold them up!' she ordered.

Most of the children obeyed, but several continued to bounce or throw them and Anna had to shout against the roaring of the wind and the distant clanging of the builders at work to make herself heard.

She showed them how to walk slowly about the playground bouncing a ball steadily, keeping it under control. It was no easy job with such numbers but most of the children seemed to enjoy this exercise. Unfortunately, Arnold and his like found this an ideal opportunity for creating havoc among the more law-abiding members, and a gentle kick at someone else's ball or a determined shove at someone's back soon caused the most pleasurable complications.

Despite such subversive elements, Anna struggled manfully on, showing the children more and more manoeuvres until the time came when she knew she must return unwillingly to the overcrowded classroom.

The box had been left under the playground shed near a long bench which was secured to the wall by steel brackets under it.

'Run and put the balls back!' called Anna unthinkingly. At once the mob pelted towards the shed. They began to pile up round the box, some shouting, some protesting that they were being squashed as they bent over the box to deposit their burdens and some flinging their balls wildly from a distance in order 'to be first back'.

It was then that Anna realized what a difference a few extra children made. If she had thought forty-eight an unmanageable mob then sixty-odd certainly made a terrifying rabble. If only, she thought guiltily, she had sent back a few at a time, or moved that wretched box into the open!

She started towards the milling and vociferous crowd and at that moment heard a high-pitched shriek. The children parted and fell back aghast.

Sitting on the ground by the bench was Michael Long, his leg outstretched. A deep gash of several inches in length poured a steady flow of blood upon the grey asphalt. To Anna's horror she saw that the wound had reached the bone and was so deep that the flesh fell away leaving a sickening bleeding trough.

The child had slipped under the bench and caught his leg against the sharp steel support under the bench. He looked pale but otherwise was remarkably calm. An unnatural hush had fallen upon the rest of the children who gathered round gazing ghoulishly at this ghastly sight.

Anna pulled herself together. A dreadful sickening attack of giddiness had seized her, but this was no time for a swooning fit, she told herself fiercely, fighting against nausea.

'Run and fetch Miss Enderby,' she told the most sensible girl present.

'She's gone out,' chorused the class. Heavens, so she had, remembered Anna!

'Miss Hobbs then,' she amended hastily. 'And run and get some mats to rest Michael on. And a rug from the sickroom!' she called after the fleeing figures, memories of first-aid classes flocking back to her.

She had never felt so pleased to see Miss Hobbs as she did on that occasion. Her sturdy figure bounded from the school door and within minutes she had taken charge.

'Take the rest in and ring the doctor, will you?' she directed. 'Four of the children can bring the stretcher and we'll carry you in, young man.'

The child smiled weakly. To Anna's relief he seemed to be feeling no pain, and almost appeared to be enjoying this unwonted attention.

Anna, much shaken, did as she was bid and before Miss Enderby returned the doctor had called, had inserted five stitches, Michael's mother had been informed, and all that remained to be done was to fill in, in triplicate, an accident form which was placed before her by Miss Hobbs's efficient hand.

But Anna could not forget the dreadful sight and could not rid herself of the terrible feeling that such accidents – and worse ones too – could happen so quickly when large numbers were in her charge. She had not quite realized, until that fateful day when Tom had been called away, how heavy her responsibilities as a teacher really were.

15. Tom Makes Plans

TOM was away for a week, and although Miss Enderby turned to and took the bereaved class as often as she could, the children had to be sent in batches to other classrooms whenever other matters engaged her attention.

Anna came to dread the sound of the approaching horde as it bumped and chattered its way towards her overcrowded room. The children were obedient, very lovable, and most anxious to win a handsome testimonial from their hostess in order to please Tom when he returned, but work went to the winds and Anna could not forget the accident whenever she led the throng gingerly to the playground.

Miss Enderby had had a reassuring telephone call from Tom on the evening of his departure, to say that the stroke had been slight and he hoped to return the next day. But during the night the old man had had a second, and more severe, attack. It was late in the afternoon, as the sun fell behind the flat fields he had cultivated so diligently and his labourers were slinging their legs across their bicycles to go home, when Tom's father died.

Tom had spent the next few days going mechanically about the dozens of jobs which had to be done. His mother was as shattered as he was himself, but both kept their feelings hidden as best they could in order to comfort the other. He sent messages to relations, arranged for the funeral at the small grey church whose spire was a landmark for many miles in this wide flat district, and did what he could to organize the market garden so that it would be easy for his mother to manage in the immediate future. He realized that his mother would like him to take over at once, but he wanted a little time to collect his dull wits, after the shock, before taking such a serious step.

Luckily, there was a reliable man who had frequently been left in charge and who was quite capable of supervising the work of the market garden.

Anna was shaken when she first saw Tom after his return. He seemed to have grown paler and older. She had missed his presence in the school more than she had cared to admit to herself, and to see him so withdrawn and tired touched her sympathetic heart.

'Is there anything I can do?' she asked shyly, when they met in the corridor and she had stammered her words of consolation.

'Yes,' said Tom. 'Come and have tea and talk to me. I'm afraid I shan't be very good company. I feel as though my head had been thoroughly kicked. But it would be a comfort if you could bear to come.'

Anna was only too glad to hear that she would be a comfort. She scribbled a note to Mrs Flynn, gave it to a child to deliver on his way home, and accompanied Tom after school to Mrs Armstrong's.

It was a blessing, thought Anna, as she sat by Tom's fire after tea, that he was so devotedly cared for by his landlady. The room was lit by the leaping flames. The furniture shone, there were hyacinths in bloom, and everywhere proclaimed the good housekeeping of kind Mrs Armstrong.

Outside the March winds howled through the twilit garden and the rain spattered the windows; but here was a haven, and although Tom still looked unusually white and forlorn, he leant back in his armchair in a more relaxed manner. There would have been nowhere for him to relax, thought Anna grimly, if he had had the misfortune to have Mrs Flynn for a landlady, and she compared the cheap, hard, fireside – and gas fireside at that! – chair in her own sitting-room with the plump comfort of the Edwardian one which now surrounded her. She realized that it would take more than soft chairs, good food, and Mrs Armstrong's motherly sympathy to cure the effects of Tom's shock, but they would all help in his recovery.

They smoked in comfortable silence for a time, watching the smoke spiral away into the shadows of the darkening room. Anna did not like to press him about his plans but he spoke of them readily enough when he threw the end of his cigarette into the flames.

'I think this settles it for me, Anna,' he said. 'I had a talk to Flo this morning and I must say she is a real trump at times like this.'

'What did she say?'

'She said she thought I should go back as soon as I could if that was what I really wanted. I should have given a month's notice, I suppose. And it is what I want, as you know, but I shan't go quite so soon.'

'Why not?' said Anna. It had been the thing he wanted more than anything else, she knew, and she was puzzled by his hesitation.

'I don't think it would be fair to Flo, for one thing. She wouldn't be able to get a replacement easily at this time of year. If I teach for the rest of this term, and next, I can see my own class through and by that time the new people will be coming out of college and it will be simpler to make an appointment.'

'But what about the market garden? And your mother?'

'My mother's sister is staying with her for as long as she likes, and Albert, who's in charge, can carry on very well until July, when I take over. I shall go down as many weekends as I can. My mother has given me father's car and that will be an enormous help. I can be home by half past six or seven on a Friday night and have time to go round the place by daylight too.'

'What does your mother think?'

'She's relieved, I believe, that I haven't thrown everything overboard at once. It gives us all time to get over things and get used to the new plans. I'm sure it's wrong to make hasty decisions when there's been a death in the family. For one thing, one's not in a fit state to make a proper judgement. I think it will be best for us all to jog gently on for a bit until we return to normal.'

For a young man, thought Anna, watching his serious face as he rearranged the coals, he is remarkably wise and sweet.

And how I shall miss him! she thought with a sudden pang.

As though he could read her thoughts, Tom suddenly smiled at her, sitting back on his heels and balancing the poker in his hand. He spoke softly.

'It isn't quite the whole story, you know, of why I'm postponing my leaving Elm Hill. There are more selfish reasons. I shall miss you most horribly, Anna.'

'Me too,' said Anna, ungrammatically, in a small husky voice.

There was a pause and Tom resumed his unnecessary attentions to the fire. His face was grave.

'This isn't the time to tell you quite how much. Too much depends on it. But I'll be glad to stay until the summer when we can see how things work out.'

He replaced the poker carefully, sighed, and then shook his head as though emerging from a cold plunge.

'Let's have some music, Anna,' he said more cheerfully, and busied himself with his gramophone.

They lay back in their chairs again as the music crept and swept about the room and Anna pondered, not for the first time, on the maddening ambiguity of the English 'we'.

'We can see how things work out,' he had said. That might mean Tom and his mother, Tom and the market gardeners, Tom and his class, Tom and his headmistress. But she hoped and believed that what he had meant was Tom and Anna Lacey.

It was soon after this that Anna found herself embroiled

with percussion band classes. Miss Enderby had brought this about much to Anna's dismay.

'There are some classes starting for teachers, dear,' she had said firmly, in a voice that boded no good. 'They are to show us how to take percussion band playing with the children. Miss Hobbs is going and I think it would be a good thing for you to go too. At the beginning of your career you must learn as much useful matter as you can.'

Anna had opened her mouth in weak protest, but Miss Enderby swept on.

'At half past five in our hall here, dear, on Tuesdays and Thursdays. Six lessons in all and nothing to pay!'

Really, thought Anna rebelliously, she makes it sound like a circus – which it probably will be. But much as she disliked the thought of returning to school twice a week for the next three weeks Anna acquiesced with as good a grace as she could muster. She had already escaped a gardening course, pottery-making classes, a Literary and Debating Circle which met weekly in the dejected little British Legion hut in the sad ruins of old Elm Hill, Keep-fit Classes, and a course on puppet-making, all pressed upon her by Miss Enderby and brought relentlessly to her notice by the innumerable papers which fluttered from the staff notice-board. She felt that percussion band classes would be a light price to pay for so much mercy in other directions, and presented herself cheerfully at five-thirty the next Tuesday, as a sacrifice upon the altar of Education.

The hall, which Anna saw crowded either with the entire school at morning assembly or with two classes for the rest of the day, seemed remarkably empty and tranquil. About two dozen chairs had been arranged in a half-circle and on them sat a motley collection of local teachers, mostly women, in depressingly utilitarian clothes.

In front an easel stood, and a young man of dainty appearance with long fair hair was busy arranging a large glossy chart over it. Beside him stood two large cardboard boxes filled with drums, tambourines, triangles, castanets, and cymbals. At least, thought Anna taking heart, we have to put those back at the end of the session and shan't have to bother about homework.

Miss Hobbs was already ensconced in the very middle of the half-circle, her sturdy brogues planted side by side and her thick skirt pulled well down round her plump calves. She was in animated conversation with a gaunt grey-faced woman in rimless spectacles, whom Anna recognized as a local headmistress and a possible rival to Miss Enderby for the post at the new school.

The headmistress nodded briefly to Anna, causing the curled ostrich feather which embraced her hat to flutter madly. Anna wondered why plain women were so addicted to fussy hats. Perhaps, like Arnold's habits, which Miss Enderby so despised, it was a compensatory impulse born of deprivation and inferiority.

She and Miss Hobbs were the only members from Elm Hill School, but Anna knew several of the teachers there by sight. Miss Hobbs was too busy talking to take much notice of her colleague, and Anna settled back to watch the dainty young man at his preparations and to listen to the conversation of two elderly ladies behind her. It was impossible not to hear them for they had both been infant teachers for over thirty years and their enunciation was exemplary.

'But *in Lent*!' one expostulated. 'I ask you, Hilda, *in Lent*! Not that it's any affair of mine, of course, what Mrs Appleby does with her daughter, but I should have thought a party could have waited!'

'It is her twenty-first,' pointed out the other, as one who is adding fuel to the fire, Anna suspected from the smug tone, rather than one who seeks to soothe.

'So what?' snapped the first. 'Plenty of other places to go to, if she must have a birthday in Lent, rather than the Church Hall.'

Anna felt a little sorry for the person who had been so thoughtless as to have been born in Lent.

'I had intended to give the girl something really nice – probably that silver fox fur of mother's that I've had by me in camphor since she died before the war – but now – no! I can't bring myself to.'

'You mustn't upset yourself over it,' said her companion, with obvious relish. 'You take it too much to heart.'

'I suppose I do,' admitted the first voice, somewhat mollified, 'but when one has Christian principles and a Christian outlook it makes one feel like shaking the girl and her stupid fat mother to hear of such downright wickedness during Lent! Lent, you know,' she persisted.

Anna was trying to reconcile the lady's Christian principles, which were obviously *her* particular prop to her self-esteem, with the severe shakings of her unfortunate neighbours which they appeared to prompt, when the young man clapped his plump pink hands, shook back a cloud of fair hair, and addressed his audience.

'Now, ladies and – gentlemen.' He flashed an arch smile at the two burly men who sat together at the end of the row and who constituted the male element in his class. They scowled back, unresponsive to this *camaraderie*.

'I want to show you the instruments first and how we hold them. This is the first and most important point.' He dived into the box at his feet and produced a tambourine.

'Come to the penitent form,' said one of the men, recovering his spirits. The young man, whose name, Anna later discovered, was Desmond Gall, threw him a coldish glance. He could give a rebuff as well as the next, it seemed to say.

'A tambourine,' said Mr Gall, holding it up with a pretty jingling. 'This is one way to use it. Another way is like this.'

He carefully threaded his left thumb into a hole in the wooden band and held the instrument edge on towards him.

The class leant forward and gazed attentively. Mr Gall raised his right hand with its fingers delicately bent.

'Then I tap it gently with just the *very tips* of my fingers,' said he, pursing his lips to show how sensitive a touch would be needed. 'Like this!'

He flicked his wrist gracefully and struck the taut skin of the tambourine a light blow.

'Penny on the drum,' said the facetious man. Mr Gall ignored him.

'Don't move the *arm*, merely the *wrist*,' cautioned Mr Gall, demonstrating the movement again.

'He's really got the loveliest nails!' Anna heard one of the ladies exclaim admiringly behind her.

The lesson continued; Mr Gall demonstrated the uses of all the instruments and then gave them one apiece to practise.

It really was most satisfying, thought Anna, tinkling happily away at a triangle, and if only the wretched thing wouldn't keep turning round and round as she was about to strike it with her little metal beater, it would be quite perfect.

She looked around her at her companions and was amused to see the rapt pleasure on their ancient countenances. Miss Hobbs was banging lustily on a side drum, while Mr Gall watched with some apprehension. Her neighbour, the angular headmistress, had a beatific smile upon her thin lips as she clashed two cymbals, violently up and down together. Anna hoped that the cutting edges were not sharp and that no one would be so foolish as to lean across the path of these implements while they were in such deadly motions.

The two Christian ladies behind her were in a fine frenzy of tambourine-shaking, their eyes sparkling with zest. What with cymbals, tambourines, triangles, drums, and castanets, all being wielded by long-repressed adults, the din was incredible. Anna was quite relieved when Mr Gall requested silence and put on a gramophone record of 'Bobby Shafto'. The school radiogram emitted its usual volley of crackles, whistles, and

rushing-wind noises, as well as the tune, but this was prefer-
able to the former cacophony.

He showed them how they would learn to read the chart
music which was draped over the easel, and he tapped his long
pointer on the brightly-coloured notes, and sang to the music
in a high light tenor. It was all most intriguing, and Anna
began to feel reconciled to her lot, after all.

For the last few minutes of the lesson the class played together, with varying degrees of accuracy. 'Bobby Shafto'
thumped noisily from the gramophone, while Mr Gall, now
pink and perspiring, his hair cascading across his forehead like
a wisp of yellow candy-floss, nodded and banged with his
pointer, and rose and fell on his toes in time to his efforts.

Miss Hobbs, purple with concentration, pummelled her
drum mercilessly, muttering the while: 'Bobby One-Two,
Bobby One-Two! Silver One-Two, At His One-Two!' one
large brogue stamping energetically on the floor. The facetious
man had met his match in a twirling triangle, which he stalked
intently holding his little beater aloft and smiting with a fine
disregard of rhythm, whenever the triangle obligingly turned
in the right direction.

It was wonderful to see two dozen grown men and women
so entranced with their own efforts, and when the lesson
ended Anna knew she looked as flushed and foolish as the rest.

As they made their way from the hall she heard the militant
Christian talking to her friend.

'Well, I did enjoy that! I think we should be very pleased
with ourselves!'

Her voice was in happy contrast to the virtuous indignation
which had sharpened it earlier that evening.

Music, Anna remembered, even such poor stuff as they had
made, still seemed to have charm to soothe the savage breast.

16. Friends and Fresh Air

THE end of term approached, and the Easter holidays, which had seemed to Anna like a distant speck of sunlight seen at the end of a long dark tunnel, suddenly shone splendidly near.

She would be heartily thankful to see the back of Elm Hill for a fortnight, she told herself. The term had been long and cold; darkness had closed in on many an afternoon session, and the drab darkness of the ruined countryside around her was enough to daunt even Anna's youthful spirits. Lack of air, sunshine, and exercise had worked upon both staff and children, and tempers had grown unpleasantly frayed.

Anna had not been prepared for adult tantrums and was shocked to see grown people bandying tart words and taking offence so easily. This was another aspect, and an unnerving one, of the career she had taken up. Her own family was particularly equable, and although she had seen her father and his farm hands, sweating with exhaustion, and occasionally blaspheming at some piece of recalcitrant machinery, they had remained basically even-tempered at their work. This edgy spitefulness, born of nervous tension, was a new and frightening thing to Anna. Would she get like that? Was she as viperish herself and didn't know it? It was an appalling thought.

She had overheard Miss Enderby, who normally kept her majestic façade unruffled, snap cruelly at poor Miss Hobbs, and the sight of Miss Hobbs's stricken face, looking like a child who has seen his mother drown his puppy, upset Anna considerably. Doubtless the strain of waiting for the new appointment to be made was taking its toll of her headmistress, thought Anna charitably.

Even Joan Berry had lost some of her cool urbanity as the

wearisome term dragged on, and Anna did not like to risk a
rebuff by asking after Maurice, though she would dearly have
loved to know if that amiable parasite was still with the same
host.

The first crocuses which had begun to flower in the raw new
gardens near the school seemed only to emphasize their bleak
and inhospitable surroundings. The stick-like lilac which
existed by Mrs Flynn's gate had put forth one or two pathetic
leaves, but the little cushions of thrift with which Mrs Flynn,
with unconscious irony, had chosen to edge the concrete path,
had died during the winter and lay, like bunches of dead hair,
in a depressing row.

Outside the blowsy greengrocer's, two or three boxes of
narcissi and daffodils huddled in their blue tissue paper, and
wilted in the dust which whipped around them every time a
lorry screamed past. Pale pink forced rhubarb, with its yellow
top-knot, arched its flabby length across the top of the boxes,
and Anna thought longingly of the sturdy growth at home
pressing up under the brown earthenware crocks in the farm
garden and awaiting her appreciative palate. Spring at Elm
Hill was a travesty of that lovely season, and it grieved her to
see her children running home along those arid streets 'missing so much and so much'. Just now, the children from the
village school would be searching the mossy banks on their
way home for white violets and brassy celandines. Birds would
be in full throat as they busied themselves with their nesting,
and over the whole sweet countryside would be the benison of
returning warmth and colour.

Anna had never felt so acutely all that she was missing, and
had never hated Elm Hill so fiercely. Mrs Flynn's parsimony
seemed to grow worse daily and Anna began to wonder if she
could bear to stay much longer in that wretched house. If she
had not been able to get away on a Friday evening for a weekend in comfort she felt that she would not have been able to
get through the term at all.

When, finally, the last day came, and the children had gone home jubilantly clutching the Easter eggs she had provided, Anna clambered on to the first Green Line coach available, threw her case thankfully on to the rack, and lay back with her eyes closed.

It was then that she realized just how exhausted she was. She felt drained of all energy, as flat and ugly as the ruined fields around her. She felt as she had when she had once been seriously ill, curiously light and empty, and quite incapable of enjoying anything.

No wonder that the older members of the staff, many of them with household cares and ill-health added to their burden, should look as they did and snap at each other, thought Anna.

And she wondered, with a spasm of fright, if she would ever be able to stick it out.

Within two days, of course, the magic of home worked its spell, and Anna was her usual buoyant self again.

The country was beginning to flower into spring. The stark black outlines of the trees took on a softer line, as though a charcoal drawing had been lightly blurred, as millions of buds swelled and began to break their tight casings. There was a rosy smoke over the elm trees, the honeysuckle, which twined over an arch in the garden, was in small bright leaf, and the rose trees had put out little red fans of new leaves. Everything smelt of hope and growing warmth and it was impossible not to respond.

Anna's pony kicked up its heels and galloped madly round the paddock for the sheer joy of living, and Anna, watching it lovingly from the kitchen window, could have joined it. It was wonderful to be young, to have a holiday, to have the summer stretching ahead. Why, even Elm Hill, at this distance, seemed quite a pleasant place!

She found that she could answer her mother's inquiries

about the job much more easily now. At first she had been so tired and so overwhelmed with the sheer ugliness of Elm Hill that she had not dared to express her true feelings for fear of upsetting her mother. But now, Elm Hill and the school were beginning to fall into place in her life, and she could talk of them more objectively.

'The staff are really jolly nice when you get to know them,' she told her mother as they prepared the large midday dinner in the kitchen. She went on to relate the story of Joan Berry's kindness to poor spineless Maurice, but carefully omitted the fact that he slept at the flat with Joan. After all, old people were easily shocked, thought Anna with newly-found sophistication, and she didn't want her mother to be embarrassed, particularly as Joan was to spend a weekend with them at the end of the holidays.

'And the children are enormous fun. Even when they're naughty,' said Anna, peeling a carrot industriously, 'it's a *nice* naughtiness – not maliciously inclined against me. Some of the bigger children, I believe, set out to be troublesome, but mine are too young for that yet.'

'And you don't find it's monotonous, teaching the same things every day?' asked her mother.

'The same things?' cried Anna. 'Why, every day's different. So many things crop up, and every child reacts in its own way, that there's always something happening. Too much, in fact, at times. You can't call teaching monotonous – if anything it's too exciting with forty-eight nine-year-olds whirling you along!'

'And you'd like to stay there?' pressed her mother. Anna lowered the carrot slowly and leant her elbows on the cool sink, gazing with unseeing eyes at the sunlit meadow beyond the quickening hedge.

'No,' she answered thoughtfully. 'Not for much longer anyway. It is marvellous experience and I'm beginning to feel that I can really teach, but after I've spent a year or so perhaps with a new head, whoever it is, I think I'll look for another post.'

'I think that might be wise,' agreed her mother, nodding sympathetically. The weariness and strain which Anna had tried to hide during the previous months had not escaped Margaret Lacey's eye, nor her husband's.

'How would you like me as headmistress of the village school here?' asked Anna, half-jokingly. 'There'll be a vacancy in the next two or three years, I should think.'

'You wouldn't get it,' said Mrs Lacey forthrightly, 'nor would you deserve it. You'd need much more experience. If you want to make a change after being at Elm Hill two or three years I should apply for a post as an assistant in a school in a country town – that is if you really think you'd like a village headship one day.'

'I think I would, you know,' said Anna slowly. 'It would probably be years ahead when I'm too old to enjoy taking the children out for nature walks and too stiff to bound about in the playground with them – but I don't think I shall ever live happily away from the country.'

Her mother laughed.

'Maybe,' she said looking at her daughter, 'you'll get married. You might possibly marry someone who lived in the country,' she added, thinking of Ted.

'So I might,' agreed Anna cheerfully, picking up the carrot again, tossing it ceilingwards and catching it again deftly. 'There's just the faintest possible chance, I suppose, that I might marry someone who lived in the country.' But she was thinking of Tom.

Joan Berry's visit was a great success. Anna's parents were instantly attracted by her gay good sense and her pretty looks, although, as Patrick Lacey told her, she 'needed to put some beef on her bones or the wind would blow her over'.

She seemed to relax and glow in the warm family atmosphere and Ted, Anna was amused to see, had eyes for no one else. He had met hosts of local girls, of varying shapes and sizes, but never before one quite so elegant and sparkling.

On the Saturday of Joan's weekend stay the local hunt held its point-to-point meeting. This took place a few miles from the Laceys' home and part of the course lay in Ted Marchant senior's fields. This was always a cheerful social occasion, when old friends met, local horses and riders were known, and everyone told everyone else the best horse to back in the next race and no one minded when it came in last.

The Laceys always made this a day's outing and the two girls helped Mrs Lacey to pack up the picnic basket during the morning. Before twelve o'clock they had parked the big shabby car in the farmers' enclosure and by twenty past Anna was not surprised to see that Ted had joined the party for lunch.

It was a wonderful April day with great white towers of

clouds sailing slowly across the wide East Anglian sky. A light easterly wind brought a hint of the distant sea, and spirits were high. Farmers and farm hands, butchers and bakers, men and women who had been cooped up in offices all the week, house-wives who had taken the day off, and hordes of excited child-ren, moved hither and thither in the brilliant sunshine, and the smell of bruised young grass was everywhere.

Ted helped Joan with her bets, poring obligingly over her race-card, as this was the first time she had been to a point-to-point. Despite his advice, Joan stuck to her own choice, and much to their delight had two unexpected winners.

'A sheer fluke really,' Ted assured her. 'Neither of them should have won.'

'Nonsense!' said Joan, 'it was purely my good eye for a horse. I knew that white one would run well.'

Ted controlled his wincings at hearing a grey so ignorantly described, with his customary good humour.

It was a happy day and Anna was delighted to see her friend looking so carefree. Maurice had not been mentioned, and it was not until the next afternoon, when the two girls had gone alone to pick primroses in a near-by copse, that Anna had the opportunity to inquire after the gentleman.

'Maurice?' said Joan, sitting back on her heels and sniffing her bunch of primroses. 'Why, he's still with me.'

'For much longer?' asked Anna. Joan laughed.

'Your guess is as good as mine. He's doing a temporary job at Fraser's, the furnishers, at the moment. Someone's ill and he's standing in, but heaven knows how long that will last.'

'Does he like it?'

'Maurice, as I've told you before, my dear, dislikes any sort of work intensely. And he finds that flinging the carpets back for prospective buyers is most exhausting!'

Anna laughed with her.

'Poor Maurice!'

'Isn't it sad?' continued Joan. 'It's as much as he can do to lift one of my gin and tonics to his pallid lips in the evenings. Terribly trying to the arms, he tells me, this carpet throwing.'

'Perhaps they'll offer him a permanent post there?'

'It won't be taken,' Joan assured her. 'If he sticks a month I shall be surprised, but I must say it's very nice to have the flat to myself a little more often. He's out most evenings.'

'At the Youth Club?' asked Anna.

'Not likely! I think he has found a sympathetic female ear somewhere and enjoys pouring out his troubles. I only hope she has more influence over him than I have, and finds him another job when this one folds up.'

She moved to another rosette of primroses and began plucking busily. Anna followed her, the brittle twigs snapping underfoot and frightening a linnet who had been singing on a silver birch tree.

She bent down to pick by her friend.

'Joan, this is perhaps rather cheek, but tell me, does Maurice – well, help towards running the flat?'

Joan did not appear in the least perturbed by Anna's faltered question.

'He does when he can. But it's all in fits and starts, you know. When he first took this job he gave me three pounds a week towards expenses, but lately it's dropped to an occasional ten shillings when he feels like it.'

'But *really* – !' began Anna indignantly, but Joan stopped her.

'I know, I know. It's idiotic of me, and it's downright wicked of Maurice, and it's all against your principles – but don't say it. I may be a perfect fool but I just can't turn that poor little wastel out into the hard world while he behaves himself at the flat. Perhaps one day I'll harden my heart, but meanwhile I'm content to let things slip on from day to day.'

'It's so absolutely wrong and unfair,' said Anna, tugging viciously at a twig of nodding catkins. Joan stopped picking primroses and straightened up, watching the younger girl with kindly amusement.

'Anna darling, you're sweet to get so worked up about it all. You see, you've been brought up so properly – and I don't mean that disparagingly, believe me. Your parents are absolutely straight and good. Not *goody-good*, but good in the wholesome honest way that crusty bread or fresh milk is good. This weekend has made me realize how lucky you are to have them as parents. You see it all still in black and white, partly because of their upbringing and partly because you are so deliciously young.'

'It doesn't alter the fact that Maurice is in the wrong,' persisted Anna.

'Maybe not,' rejoined Joan. 'But because I'm older and have met so many less good people than you have, I expect less from them. The more you know people the more readily you can forgive their weaknesses.'

'My mother says that,' agreed Anna wonderingly.

'Bless her, she would!' responded Joan warmly. 'And another thing, I'm terribly lazy. I'd sooner let things drift on than make a scene unnecessarily. That's why I let so many comments go by me in the staff room. If one took up every double-edged remark – particularly towards the end of term – one would be in a constant state of warfare!'

Anna, remembering those uncomfortable last few days, nodded agreement.

'What will you do if Miss Enderby goes to the new infants' school?' she asked Joan, her mind wandering back to Elm Hill. They had reached a wide glade, threaded with April sunlight, where they could walk comfortably side by side.

'I shall go with her if she'll have me,' said Joan stoutly. 'She's a grand old girl, you know, beneath that lady-of-the-manor attitude she takes up to us underlings.'

'She is,' said Anna, and told her about the forthright way she had dealt with Mrs Bond on her behalf. 'I suppose she's just used to coping with crises like that. She must have had all sorts of experiences. And unhappiness too,' added Anna, 'she looks terribly sad when she looks at that ring.'

Joan's laughter sent a blackbird scuttling for shelter.

'Bless your romantic young heart,' said she, 'I shall have to tell you the truth about that ring, though I'd told myself I'd keep it locked for ever in my black heart.'

'Sit on this log,' commanded Anna, taking her place promptly, 'and tell me quickly.'

'Well,' began Joan, her eyes sparkling, 'I met a Miss Evans some time ago when I was on holiday. She had been to college with Flo and they had taught together in Wolverhampton, until this Elm Hill headship had whisked them apart. Having always been unholily inquisitive about that ring I spoke of it to Miss Evans, who said –'

Here she paused tantalizingly and turned her bright gaze upon Anna's absorbed face.

'Go on! Go on!' pressed Anna.

'Who said,' continued Joan, with tormenting deliberation, 'that Flo had been left a little money by an aunt and had decided to buy that ring with some of it. In fact, she accompanied Flo to the shop and helped her to choose it. In those days she did *not* wear it on her engagement ring finger.'

'Well, I'm blowed!' said Anna inelegantly. 'What a thing! Do you think that story's true?'

'I don't see any reason for doubting it,' said Joan equably. 'She was a nice old dear, and not likely to perjure her immortal soul for my passing gratification.'

'But it's downright dishonest, if that's the case,' said Anna, beginning to see the enormity of the situation. 'I mean Flo's as good as telling a whopping great lie by letting us all believe that she was engaged once!'

'Calm down, junior,' said Joan. 'There you go again, you see. Of course, it's wrong. Of course, Flo shouldn't behave like that, but she does. And I, for one, can forgive a pathetic little sin like that quite easily. Believe you me, some of my own are pretty formidable beside that tiddy-widdly one of Flo's.'

'I wish,' said Anna slowly, 'that I were as kindhearted as you.'

'It's my great age,' answered Joan lightly, giving her companion an encouraging pat on the shoulder. 'It makes me mellow and worldly-wise, you know. Wait another five years and you'll be just as big-hearted!'

They picked up their bunches of yellow primroses and set off towards the farmhouse.

'Yes, I'll stay with Flo,' repeated Joan as they came out of the wood and paused to look upon the open countryside spread around them. 'I admire the old battle-axe tremendously. She's got pluck. She's hard-working, she knows what she wants, and she commands respect – ring or no ring. If she gets the headship that school will be jolly well run. She hasn't really had a chance to show her form, we've been so hopelessly overcrowded.'

'I think I'll stay on, with the juniors,' said Anna. 'I like the older children better than the infants, I think, and a new head would be more experience for me but in surroundings I'm just getting used to.'

'We'd still see plenty of each other,' said Joan. 'The two schools will work together, I imagine, quite a bit. I must say I'm looking forward to Elm Hill being spread out. We can really enjoy our teaching then.'

Anna looked at her with quick interest.

'Tell me, after five years at it,' said Anna, 'do you really enjoy teaching?'

'Yes, I do,' maintained Joan stoutly. 'It gets better every year I go on. I know it's unfashionable these days to admit to enjoying children's company and to working with them, but I find teaching stimulating and amusing and jolly well worthwhile. It gives me the biggest kick in the world to see a child reading itself a story when I know that last week it could hardly put two words together without effort. Just think what's begun for that child!'

'That's cheering news!' said Anna, quickening her pace as the farmhouse came in sight.

'You don't want to believe all that you read in the library books,' continued Joan. 'Remember, my child, that for every disgruntled teacher who has burst into dismal print, there are two dozen cheerful ones who are far too busy weeding their gardens or baking a cake in their spare time, to ponder on their hard lot. And praise the Lord for that!'

As they approached the farmhouse a delicious smell of cooking floated towards them.

'Someone,' said Anna jubilantly, 'has been doing some baking in *our* house, evidently!'

Together they approached the kitchen door at a smart trot.

17. Testing Time

THE summer term was going to be mightily disturbed, it seemed to Anna on the first day back, as she stood in front of the staff notice-board reading a long list which Miss Hobbs had just put up.

> 4 May Verse-Speaking Competition
> 5 May Choral Competition
> 15 June Open Day
> 13 July School Sports Day
> 20 July Area Sports Day

So ran the list, headed in Miss Hobbs's firm hand, 'Dates to Note'.

'Don't expect to get any real work done this term,' said Joan Berry, as Miss Hobbs bustled off. 'The summer term's an absolute nightmare.'

'There are only five dates,' replied Anna reasonably. 'Surely they can't make much difference.'

'Dear, innocent, muddle-headed child,' said Joan, looking up from her minute diary in which she had been putting down the dates. 'Just think for one second. All those wretched events need weeks of practice and rehearsal. Open Day alone, at Elm Hill, shortens one's life by six months, I reckon. This year, with Flo in the last stretch of the New School Stakes, it will be even worse!'

'But what happens?' asked Anna, bewildered. 'Surely it simply means that the parents come to see the work?'

'And what work!' commented Joan darkly. 'All the cleanest bits of needlework, all the maddest pictures in the which-way-up style, all the fanciest maps, and so on, that your children have perpetrated through the year, will need to be exquisitely

mounted on black paper – if the stock-cupboard runs to it –
and carefully displayed. No ramming of marguerites into a
Virol jar that day, my girl! Something worthy of Constance
Spry has to decorate each window-sill and the cupboards must
be models of tidiness!'

'Oh Lor'!' said Anna appalled.

'A few beautifully printed poems in your own best Marion
Richardson hand will be expected to add a touch of culture to
your walls, and I suppose I shall be spending the next six weeks
making a madly gay alphabet frieze for my babies' room. And
I'd better replace my notices for DOOR, CUPBOARD, and so
on,' she continued morosely. 'I've had them for six years and
all the corners are bent. Besides cream is out just now. A good
bright scarlet might win approval. I must put in my claim for
stock pretty quickly, and I advise you to do the same, my
dear, before Flo is besieged by the rest of the staff. As it is, you
know, she hates parting with the stuff. All stock-cupboard
minders get that way. It's an occupational hazard.'

'Thanks, I will,' said Anna. 'What an outlook though,' she
added. 'Is it really as bad as that?'

'Worse!' said Joan cheerfully. 'Much worse – but I don't
like to depress you by telling you more just now.'

Anna knew that Joan's remark about Miss Enderby's fru-
gality with stock was a true one. Every week it was the custom
for each teacher to send to Miss Enderby a list of stock needed
for class work. It usually ran something like this:

12 Arithmetic exercise books
12 Writing books
12 Sheets painting paper
24 Sheets baker's wrapping paper
      (used for crayoning and pencil work)
12 Pencils
Plasticine
Drawing pins

The last two items, Anna had found by sad experience, were best left in their stark form, for if any number of sticks of plasticine were mentioned or a whole box of drawing pins were asked for, Miss Enderby seemed to feel obliged to cut down supplies drastically.

There seemed to be something malevolent about the stock-cupboard's influence, Anna thought. Normally, Miss Enderby was an open-handed person. She delighted in presenting the staff room with flowers. Sometimes she gave a cake for her grateful staff to eat with their afternoon tea. But once in the stock cupboard she became parsimonious. Paper of most kinds she seemed to find comparatively easy to part with, but rare commodities such as thick black paper for mounting work, gummed coloured squares, so useful for cutting-out, and particularly drawing-pins she seemed most reluctant to hand out.

'I buy my own,' said Tom Drew, when Anna spoke of this particular foible of her headmistress's, one day. 'To see the spasm of pain which contorts the poor old girl's face, when I ask for a few miserable drawing-pins, is too much for my susceptible heart. It's worth a bob a term to feel magnanimous.'

With Joan's advice in mind, Anna went with some trepidation to collect her stock on the first day the cupboard was unlocked. Her list had been formidably long and included those vital drawing pins. Luckily, Miss Enderby was in an unusually benevolent mood and handed out great rolls of heavy paper, sticks of coloured chalk, and a dozen new pencils which Anna had not dared to ask for, as well as a whole new box of drawing pins. Anna congratulated herself silently on having applied early and at such a propitious time. Success made her brave enough to make a comment on the stock available.

'It must be awfully difficult to know how much you will need of everything,' she said, eyeing the shelves.

'One gets used to estimating,' answered Miss Enderby graciously, disentangling her hair-net from a hank of raffia which dangled from a high nail. 'This is the last term of the three. I shall order ready for next term, of course, for my own needs or those of my successor here.'

'I hadn't thought of that,' said Anna truthfully.

'The new school will need stock, too, but of course the new head will put in her order for that.'

'Of course,' echoed Anna, clutching her unwieldy goods to her cardigan. Miss Enderby's gaze had wandered to the window and to the distant prospect of Elm Hill Infants' School. The roof was now on, and the sounds of building were mainly from inside and mercifully muffled. She seemed to have forgotten Anna and a heavy silence fell.

Anna looked at her list and found that she had received all that she had requested.

'Thank you very much, Miss Enderby,' she murmured politely, backing quietly away with her spoils. But Miss Enderby did not seem to hear, and Anna guessed that she was already, in spirit, standing in another stock cupboard, filled with the bright necessities of an infants' school, and all of her own ordering.

But before the first of Miss Hobbs's 'Dates To Note' materialized, a more momentous day occurred for Anna.

She had hoped that the worst of her probationary troubles were now over. She had been visited by half a dozen or so educational advisers, of much the same kidney as Miss-Adams-of-the-rods, and felt that she had learnt something from their varied, and sometimes mildly fanatical suggestions.

Miss Enderby too had been a model headmistress in her handling of her new member of staff. She had come into many of Anna's lessons, sitting, as unobtrusively as a woman of her size and presence could, in a far-too-small desk at the back of the room. Afterwards she had given very fair comment on her findings and Anna had found her experience of considerable help. Miss Enderby was zealous too in examining Anna's

'Record Book' weekly. This large volume consisted of a list of subjects against which Anna made a note of the work scheduled to be done each week, so that against 'Nature', for instance, she might have: 'Hibernating Animals – Hedgehog and Squirrel.'

Too often, alas, Anna found that the heading would remain the same for two or three weeks running; for although she might have planned to have three weeks' lessons on hibernating animals, and had mentally reserved the toad, the snake, and the tortoise for one week and bats and dormice for the last, yet the pressure and upheaval of school life often ousted a lesson completely from one week's work, and it had to be carried into the next. It was her record book which gave Anna some idea of the loss of time which out-of-class interruptions occasioned. Unexpected visitors, rehearsals for plays, fire drill, searches for lost property, and dozens of other school hazards seemed to take their toll of Anna's carefully prepared lessons. The record book was both her bane – for she sometimes forgot to make it up and earned a rebuke from her headmistress – and also her prop, for with a dozen or more subjects to teach Anna often found that her head was in a whirl, and she was glad to refer to her notes to straighten her thoughts.

She had received three or four visits from inspectors, of varying degrees of helpfulness, and sincerely hoped that there were to be no more. The rest of the staff were not so optimistic.

'I'd count on half a dozen,' said Joan Berry, experimenting with gold nail varnish one playtime. She held up one finger and looked at it critically. 'What do you think of this?'

'Well –' began Anna doubtfully.

'Awful!' said Tom Drew. 'It looks like tobacco stain. Stick to the pink.'

'I believe you're right,' agreed Joan, wiping it off. 'Yes, my dear,' she resumed, 'you must expect a little visitation or two in your last term. The pace gets hotter when the tape's in sight.'

'I had a holy terror,' said Tom conversationally. 'He asked me if I could teach a class a dovetail joint and how would I set about explaining the Trinity. It was a trifle disconcerting.'

'Watch out for one called Butterworth, or Shuttleworth, or some such name,' warned Joan, screwing up the bottle of nail varnish. 'He throws the children up to the ceiling and tells them uproarious stories and generally gets them into a state of screaming hysteria and then he says: "Carry on."'

Anna's eyes widened in horror.

'Quite true!' Tom assured her, smiling at her solemn face. 'He likes to see how quickly you can restore order. Carries a stop-watch, doesn't he, Joan?'

'That's right,' agreed Joan. 'If you can get control in ten seconds flat, you're in.'

'Don't you believe a word of it, Miss Lacey,' puffed Alan Foster, who had entered and was busy spreading papers at one end of the table. 'Nothing to fear from inspectors. I was talking to one yesterday about this little project.' He waved at the mass of material before him. 'He was most interested. Said that a really worthwhile arithmetic series is exactly what's needed in the junior schools today.'

The three younger members gathered round Alan Foster's bulk and gazed at his latest work. Through the haze of cigarette smoke, which spiralled round his bald head, Anna stared at innumerable diagrams and columns of figures. It looked very much like all the other arithmetic books she had met. Alan Foster smiled proudly at it.

'Well, there it is! Good for five hundred pounds, I'd say, within the first two years, and a steady income for the rest of my life.'

'Let's hope so,' said Tom dubiously, as the bell rang. 'You're staying here for a free period, I suppose?'

'Yes,' said Alan, patting a few papers together in an efficient manner. 'I shall put in half an hour on this while I can.'

'Poor old Alan,' Tom commented to Anna as they walked

together back to their classrooms. 'I doubt if putting together "many cheerful facts about the square on the hypotenuse" is going to make his fortune, but it seems to keep him happy.'

He turned into his own classroom and Anna continued along the passage to her own. The class sounded remarkably quiet, and when she entered she saw why.

A large elderly man, with forbidding black eyebrows, stood at the back of the room. In his hand he held one of the children's exercise books.

He did not appear to like what he saw in it, and Anna's heart sank.

'My name is North,' he said, coming towards the front of the room. 'You are Miss Lacey, I believe?'

'Yes,' faltered Anna, her eyes on the exercise book. What had she left undone there, she wondered? Whether it was Mr North's unsmiling countenance, his bass voice, or her own guilty conscience which produced her unusual inner qualms, Anna was not sure, but she had not felt so nervous with her other visitors. Perhaps the alarm felt by older members of the staff was infectious. In any case, she found herself decidedly frightened and despised herself for feeling so.

'Set them to work,' said Mr North. 'I've one or two things to ask you.'

This sounded even more ominous. At least he's not the one who wants dovetail joints and the Trinity explained, thought Anna, clinging to a straw.

She told her class to read silently or to work in their 'busy books' while she was engaged with their visitor, and was thankful to see that they set about their task in an unusually subdued way. Evidently Mr North's dour presence flung a shadow over the children's volatile spirits as well as their teacher's.

'Just look at this, will you?' asked Mr North, handing over

the exercise book, when comparative peace had fallen upon the classroom.

He pointed to some corrections which Anna had blithely ticked. It was one of Miss Enderby's rules that a spelling mistake or a word wrongly used should be corrected by the teacher and copied three times by the child.

'My brother went to', had run the original sentence, which Anna had corrected to 'too'. Alas, the child had copied 'to' 'to' 'to', industriously at the end of his exercise, and poor

Anna, in the press of work, had ticked it as correct. It was unforgivable, she knew, but did it really call for the solemnity of Mr North's countenance? Miserably she acknowledged her fault. Mr North's expression grew, if anything, rather more grave.

'It may seem a little thing to you,' he said heavily, 'but that child might well go through life using that word wrongly. You may find people – colleagues of mine even – who profess to despise corrections in English work. I don't. I think that the pendulum has swung too far and that too much slipshod writing has resulted.'

Anna nodded dumbly. There was not much she could say in extenuation, and if it gave him any gratification to air his opinions, she was in no position to protest. Arnold, she noticed with some alarm, had cut out a paper mask for himself decorated with horrible crossed eyes and eyebrows uncommonly like Mr North's. The resourceful child had cut a large aperture for the mouth through which he protruded his tongue, all the more horrific as it was bright purple from licking an indelible pencil.

Luckily, Mr North had seated himself on the front desk, with his back to the class, and Anna prayed that Arnold would be either unobserved or, better still, smitten by an unobtrusive bolt from heaven and taken from their midst.

'How long do you spend in going through an exercise like this?' persisted Mr North, rubbing a thick finger along the black brows and turning them into herringbone stitch.

'It takes me about an hour and a half, I suppose,' answered Anna. 'It depends of course on how much they've done. Forty-eight books take a long time to mark,' she added apologetically.

'Forty-eight children are too many, of course,' said Mr North casually, 'but there it is. You're no worse off than hundreds of others, deplorable as it is.'

Anna suddenly felt furious with him and all her other tormentors who had so glibly expressed dissatisfaction with the huge numbers, but did not really seem to realize all that it involved. My goodness, thought Anna warmly, if his wife were asked to mind just one child for just one afternoon it would be something to think about, and yet teachers are expected, not only to *mind*, but to *teach* forty or more, week after week and year after year, and no one thinks it remarkable at all!

'I'd like to see your record book and any notes of lessons you may have,' went on Mr North. 'What are they supposed to be doing now?'

'I usually tell them a story,' said Anna weakly.

'Then carry on,' said Mr North, in a doom-laden voice. Anna handed over the books he had asked for, and with a sinking heart, told the children to put away their work and get ready to listen. Arnold, she was relieved to see, had been robbed of his mask by his neighbour who, with considerable aplomb, was sitting on it. Arnold, scarlet in the face with suppressed wrath, was powerless to budge him, and though Anna feared that ugly recriminations might ensue she hoped that these might be postponed until playtime.

She began the story haltingly. She was in the throes of telling her class some Greek legends and today's was the story of Theseus and the Minotaur. She prided herself on being able to tell, rather than read, the stories, for she had found that the children listened much more eagerly. But today her nervousness made her falter and the children seemed bored. Mr North had ensconced himself on a radiator by the window and was studying the notebooks gloomily. Occasionally he made a note of his own with a very small pencil on a very small pad and looked even more morose as he did so.

Anna found it heavy going that afternoon. The clock seemed to have stopped, so slowly did the time go. The children yawned and gave sidelong glances at their silent and unsmiling visitor whenever he cleared his throat with a noise like the last trump.

At last the story drew to an end, and Mr North rose and approached Anna again. He held out a large cold hand in farewell. His dark eyes stared resignedly into Anna's.

'Good-bye, Miss Lacey,' he said heavily. 'Just do the best you can.'

And with these inspiring words he vanished from Anna's sight.

'So you've been closeted with our Mr Rochester, have you?' said Joan Berry. 'Happy little fellow, isn't he?'

'Poor chap,' said Andy Craig. 'Lives on stomach powders, I heard. Just a mass of ulcers.'

'So shall I be if he comes much more,' retorted Anna. 'He's the most unnerving person I've ever met. I don't like to think what he's put in his little notebook about me.'

'Cheer up,' said Andy Craig, tightening his wrist strap. 'Teachers are in short supply, you know. You won't get thrown out.'

The hubbub of children at play which had accompanied this conversation was suddenly and unnaturally stilled, and in the lull Anna could hear Tom Drew's voice in the playground. She knew he was on duty and went to the window to see what was happening.

Tom was addressing Arnold and his class neighbour. Both were hot and angry. Arnold's nose was dripping blood and a bruise was rapidly rising on his opponent's forehead. Recriminations were now taking place evidently.

'Ah well,' said Anna thankfully, 'it might have been a lot worse!'

18. The Muse Visits Elm Hill

ANOTHER crisis arose about this time at Mrs Flynn's. It had been apparent to Anna, for some time, that her use of the sitting-room was increasingly irksome to Mrs Flynn. If her bedroom had been larger she would have suggested having a table or desk there to do her work in the evenings, for now that early summer had arrived, it was not so bitterly cold in her little cell, but it was quite impossible to jam any more furniture in it, at the moment, and Anna had endured, in silence, one or two veiled hints at the inconvenience caused by giving up the sitting-room, not knowing quite what to do about it.

Matters came to a head when Mrs Flynn entered one evening, rather flushed about the face and neck, and looking more than usually militant.

Anna guessed her errand.

'I'm afraid I shall have to ask you to give up this room entirely, Miss Lacey,' said Mrs Flynn abruptly. 'My husband said I must speak to you about it.' (Oh how useful husbands can be! thought Anna.)

'I'm sorry,' she said aloud. 'I know it must be difficult for you.'

'*Very* difficult,' said Mrs Flynn swiftly. 'Now we're getting to know more people in Elm Hill we find we must have this room to entertain them. Why, only yesterday, when you were out at tea with young Mr Drew, Mrs Porter called in – the one you met at my tea-party, remember?'

Anna did indeed remember the velvet pancake hat above the vast marshmallow face.

'And I had to ask her into the dining-room just as I'd taken tea in. And it was sprats at that!' she added bitterly.

Anna was about to ask what was wrong with a good healthy sprat, lightly fried, but noticing Mrs Flynn's apparent chagrin, thought better of it.

'It would have been all the same, as I said to Mr Flynn when she'd gone, if she'd brought her friend Lady Parr with her. Anyway, that decided it.'

'I quite understand,' said Anna. 'But you can see my difficulty. I really have nowhere to work.'

'You'll have to manage with the top of the dressing table,' said Mrs Flynn, rising. 'Unless you prefer to get other lodgings, of course,' she added tartly.

Anna would have preferred it, but knew only too well how hard it would be to find others. She decided to temporize.

'We'll see how things work out,' she said slowly. 'Maybe I can stay late at school one or two evenings.'

But as she watched Mrs Flynn tug at the intractable door she had already made up her mind that she must seek lodgings elsewhere, and her spirits rose at the thought, though cold reason did its best to damp them down.

Now that Tom had his father's car he and Anna were more adventurous on their occasional outings. They had been to the theatre once or twice, which had been difficult to do when relying on public transport, and more frequently drove out into near-by Buckinghamshire and then enjoyed a long walk in the fresh country air after being imprisoned in the classroom.

As the evenings grew lighter they went further afield, and it was on one of these happy occasions that Anna told Tom about looking for new lodgings.

'I'd already thought of it,' said Tom. Anna looked at him in open-mouthed surprise.

'And so had Mrs Armstrong,' continued Tom calmly. 'She thinks that you're being hopelessly exploited at Mrs Flynn's, and so do I. And if you like the idea, she suggests that you take over my digs when I leave.'

'*Like* the idea!' almost shouted Anna. 'There's nothing I'd like more! It's absolutely perfect!'

Tom seemed delighted at her reaction.

'Let's go straight back,' Anna rattled on, 'and tell Mrs Armstrong how much I'd love it. It was good of her to think of me.'

In point of fact, it was Tom who had thought of it and suggested it to Mrs Armstrong. She was only too pleased to agree. The rooms were there to be let, she liked Anna, and was sorry for the girl in her present circumstances. She was sorrier still for Tom who, she guessed, was sad enough at heart in leaving Anna behind, even if it were only for a little while, and who would be somewhat comforted to know that she was being left in good hands.

Anna's relief was great. She had dreaded tramping the blowsy streets of Elm Hill, mounting unknown staircases, and battling with hard-faced landladies. Now it was all resolved for her, and the thought of Mrs Armstrong's warm comfortable house and her lavish table was inexpressibly cheering.

'I was beginning to wonder where on earth I'd be next term,' confessed Anna. 'It can be horribly depressing in the autumn at Elm Hill. But I shall be so snug at Mrs Armstrong's with a real fire with logs, and your comfortable armchair – I quite look forward to next winter now!'

'In fact,' said Tom, with a grave face, 'you'll really prefer my room to my company.'

'Oh, of *course* not!' said Anna vehemently, falling into the trap, 'I shall miss you terribly, and wish you were there too.'

'Thank you, kind child,' said Tom, 'though I did have to prompt you! In any case I shall come back often – very often. You know that surely?'

'I hope you will,' said Anna soberly.

'Of course I shall,' said Tom. 'And in any case,' he added primly, 'Mrs Armstrong has invited me particularly!'

*

The verse-speaking and choral competitions were now upon them, and Elm Hill, in company with a dozen or more primary schools, had entered teams for this two-day event which took place in the Town Hall.

Anna's presence was not required at the choral day, but as two of her class were entered for the verse-speaking competition, she was to take her children to hear the contestants.

Miss Hobbs had been in charge of the training, which she conducted with the same forthright vigour with which she took her 'Rhythmic Work' classes. For the past few weeks peremptory summonses had arrived at Anna's desk requesting the immediate attendance of Freda Carter and Gabrielle Pugg, the red-haired door monitor, at a rehearsal. At least, thought Anna, as the day of the competition dawned, that's one interruption less to face each day.

The morning was sparkling-bright. The 'ever-changing panorama of the heavens' which arched so magnificently above the sordid pettiness of Elm Hill, was alight with shining, fast-moving, white clouds. A brisk wind, albeit tinged with sulphurous fumes from the near-by gas-works, raised the spirits, and the thought of getting out of the frying-pan of the classroom, even if it were into the fire of the Town Hall, was invigorating.

All the junior teachers were busy in the cloakrooms seeing that their charges were well wrapped up for the half-mile walk, that socks were pulled up, shoe-laces tied, and coats properly buttoned, so that Elm Hill School should appear before the public gaze as a credit to its name and its headmistress. Miss Enderby herself, in a new green suit and elegant black hat surmounted by cocks' feathers, led the party out of the school gates and towards the distant arena.

The journey was not without incident, as might be expected. The infants had been left behind, but even so half Elm Hill School presented a formidably long crocodile winding its way along the new pavements and across rutted unmade roads.

Arnold had to be publicly reprimanded for helping himself to a spray of cherry blossom overhanging the pathway. Miss Hobbs, a prey to agitation, had forgotten to bring the seating plans for the hall and was forced to rush back down the length of the column to retrieve them from school, brushing aside all offers of help. Gabrielle Pugg, in an advanced state of nerves, was threatened with nose-bleeding, and made the journey with a handkerchief clutched against her face, like some poor unfortunate who has just escaped from the dentist's clutches.

It was a relief to get inside the murky Town Hall, despite its cold musty odour, and to find themselves ranged at the side of the great hall under the balcony which ran round three sides. Miss Hobbs, still perspiring from her exertions, collected her team in one special row and sat guarding them like a jealous bulldog. Gabrielle Pugg sat next to her, her head thrown back, while Miss Hobbs applied cold pennies to the nape of her neck, and called last-minute advice to the rest of the row, in a voice that could have successfully raised the dead.

Anna saw that the adjudicators were ranged at a large table on a dais at the back of the hall, facing the stage. There were three men and three women, a jumble of papers, handbags, spectacles, a glass of water, and a microphone. This was certainly more fun than arithmetic, thought Anna pleasurably, and settled back, on her uncomfortable bench, to enjoy this day's outing.

The first school to file self-consciously on to the stage was St Matthew's, a near neighbour of Elm Hill, but housed in a grimy block not far from the station. Anna had looked upon its black walls, and its arid yard enclosed behind high rusty railings, and had thanked her stars that her appointment had not been there.

St Matthew's selected verse-speaking group placed themselves neatly on the platform. They had been arranged in height and made a goodly show, their dazzling white socks catching the eye and leading it to the neat grey tunics or suits above. Their faces, all uniformly pink and gleaming with soap, registered a variety of expressions, ranging from frank alarm to smug self-importance. Their teacher, arrayed in her best navy-blue suit, with an edging of pink petticoat showing, faced them from a small dais. Her back was towards the audience, but it was quite apparent that she was rallying her band by the answering flickers and half-smiles which played upon her charges' features.

The first poem chosen by this school was:

> Said the wind to the Moon, 'I will blow you out!'
>   'You stare
>   In the air
>   Like a ghost in a chair,
>   Always looking what I am about –
>   I hate to be watched; I'll blow you out.'

It had never been one of Anna's favourites, and by the time St Matthew's had finished with it, she doubted if she would ever be able to face it again. Alas, it seemed more than likely that she would have to do so several times that morning, for only four poems had been put forward for selection. Two had to be chosen and it seemed, from the disparaging comments of the school behind her, that this same poem had also been chosen by them to impress the judges.

St Matthew's school had put such a wealth of expression, both of voice and countenance, into their rendering that Anna wondered how their hard-working teacher could bear it at such close quarters. Never was there such shooting forward of lips for 'moon' and 'blow' and 'out'. Never was there such vehemence as that projected into the phrase 'I hate to be watched'. There was even a concerted stamp of right legs, a uniform flashing of white socks, on the word 'hate'.

Anna felt too embarrassed to watch, and was astounded at the barrage of applause which greeted the end of this interminable ordeal. St Matthew's filed off, beaming with pride and relief, and the adjudicators conferred busily at the rostrum.

The second entry was a group from a school near the Buckinghamshire border, and they had chosen to recite 'Five Eyes'.

Despite their own and their teacher's endeavours, there remained a comforting Buckinghamshire flavour to their vowel sounds, so that the title rang out: 'Foive Oyes' and the words 'noit' and 'broight' ran with pleasant homeliness in Anna's ears attuned to country voices.

Not so their successors, whose diction was so genteel that 'Faive Ayes' was only the prelude to a painful few minutes of tortured vowel sounds. Their pink, obedient little jaws dropped so zealously that Anna had some difficulty in recognizing:

'Then dah-oon they pah-oonce, nah-oo in nah-oo ah-oot,' for the line it really was.

Elm Hill, she knew, had chosen 'Berries', and when their turn came she was amazed to find how nervous she was on their behalf. But she need have had no fears. Miss Hobbs's broad back, solidly resplendent in brown dog-tooth check, gave one a wonderful feeling of confidence. Gabrielle Pugg had quite recovered and stood in the middle of the front row, her red hair, green eyes, and raw pink nose all aflame.

They got off to a flying start and romped along in cheerful unison. Miss Hobbs had trained them well, thought Anna, and was delighted that their effort was so well received.

The morning wore on. The Town Hall grew stuffier and stuffier, despite some cruel draughts from nine massive windows set very high in the walls, each depicting one of the Muses in regrettable stained glass. The lunch break was more than welcome.

Sandwiches were provided for everybody, the teachers having collected payment beforehand for this refreshment, and while Anna was looking doubtfully at a very thick sandwich with an unidentifiable filling, Tom loomed up beside her.

'Come and have something at The Three Feathers,' he said. 'Flo says we're all to get some air for a few minutes. She's going to hold the fort.'

Anna thankfully accompanied him into the bright May morning. Somewhere, above the wasteland, a lark was singing, trickling forth a cascade of bright notes as pure and clear as icy water. Anna tilted her head up to look at it, screwing up her eyes against the dazzling sunlight.

'Doesn't it make you long to rush back to the country?' she cried.

Tom looked at her, as she stood against a background of mean houses, moving traffic, and the distant factory chimneys which lined the horizon.

'You'll be there very soon,' he promised.

Pleasantly replete, Anna returned to the afternoon session in a state of semi-somnolence. The sun, filtered through the nine Muses, cast a variety of colours upon the hundreds sitting in the hall and, Anna watching their slow-moving beams, felt as though she were one of many tiny stones in the depths of some huge kaleidoscope.

The poems followed hard on the heels of each other. The wind blew the moon, the old woman picked blackberries, and the miller's three cats continued to pounce, occasionally giving way to an interlude for the fourth poem, which was:

'Art thou poor, yet hast thou golden slumbers?' one which, Anna decided, fitted her own case very neatly.

A professional *diseuse*, of hideous gauntness, gave a short recital of modern poems, which gave a pleasant breathing-space to the afternoon's labours, and if one closed one's eyes, Anna decided, the result was unalloyed pleasure.

The judges' comments and the awarding of places ended the day's competition and Elm Hill came second. Miss Hobbs, pink and breathless with delight, bore off a silver cup with a lid which did not quite fit, and everyone returned home in the greatest good spirits.

'How did it go?' asked Joan Berry the next day. It was the dinner hour and she and Anna were alone in the babies' room which was Joan's domain.

'Very well,' answered Anna, and proceeded to tell her all about the competition, while Joan searched through her huge new calf handbag for a lipstick.

'Drat these new-shaped bags!' said Joan, lifting out the contents and dumping them on her desk. 'Can never find a thing! Everything you want falls to the bottom. Next time I'll buy one with pockets and zips and compartments, like my mother uses.'

She took out a letter with the next assorted handful and Anna could not help noticing, with a shock of surprise, that the envelope was addressed in young Ted's unmistakable hand.

He habitually used a very fine nib and black ink and had a spidery ornate style inherited from his first school-mistress, who had been an elderly Frenchwoman. It was strangely out of keeping with Ted's large strong hands that they should wield such a ladylike pen.

Anna's narrative faltered as she averted her gaze from the letter, but Joan did not seem aware of it. She found her lipstick, plied it vigorously and replaced her property without comment.

'Is Maurice still with you?' asked Anna, for something to say. Joan's bright mouth took on a grim line.

'He won't be after tonight,' she said, with unusual force.

'Frankly, I'm jolly glad to hear it,' said Anna. 'You know how I've felt.'

'Well,' said Joan, 'I hadn't intended to spill the beans to anyone, but it would be quite a relief to get it off my chest if you could bear with me for a few minutes.'

'You know I'm all agog,' said Anna. 'It's like a serial story for me – though I know it's a good deal more than that for you, poor darling.'

Joan settled back in her hard chair, put her elegant legs up on the desk and lit a cigarette. She appeared calm, but Anna noticed that her eyes were troubled and her hand shook as she held her lighter. What had that wretched Maurice done to upset her so?

'I told you that something definite would have to happen to make me tough enough to sling Maurice out into the snow. Well, it's happened. I'm pretty sure he's pinched some money of mine.'

'No!' said Anna, aghast.

'My own fault, I suppose,' said Joan, flicking ash at the waste-paper basket under the desk. 'You know what a curse it is to get to the banks when you're teaching. They're closed after school and it cuts into the dinner hour to go then, and if you leave it till Saturday morning it's one mad spurt to fit in the shopping and washing the week's smalls before the banks close at twelve, so I normally make one sortie and keep rather a lot of money loose at home.'

'Don't you lock it up?' asked Anna.

'Not since poor old Hobbs had her month's wages pinched and a Queen Anne bureau bashed up into the bargain! No, I stuff five quid among my corsets and another five among the gloves, and a few notes in my desk drawer and some in my wallet – you know the sort of thing – but of course it was a temptation to a broken reed like Maurice. His new girl is rather predatory, I gather. I think he needs a lot of money at the moment.'

'But he's earning now –' protested Anna.

'Obviously not enough,' commented Joan. 'In any case, five pounds has disappeared overnight from my glove drawer, and I think the odd note or two has been vanishing here and there for the past few weeks, but I can't be sure.'

'I can lend you some money,' Anna said, 'if you're short.'

Joan squeezed her hand affectionately.

'Bless you, my child, but I'm still solvent. The maddening thing is that I'd seen an amethyst clip which I felt I must have. Well, now I shall just have to do without, I suppose. At least it's played its part – I feel so savage, when I think of it, I could throw Maurice out of a top window with one hand tied behind me!'

'Don't relent!' exhorted Anna, delighted to see the fires of righteous wrath so kindled in her friend. 'Do it tonight! My goodness, it should have happened months ago.'

'So everyone says, including your nice Ted,' said Joan.

'How did he know?' asked Anna. 'I didn't breathe a word.'

'I told him one day in an expansive moment,' confessed Joan. 'We've met twice in town. He's been up about some farm machinery once or twice, and he's a comforting sort of fellow to pour out one's heart to. He offered to throw Maurice out for me immediately. Said he'd simply love to!'

'He would too,' said Anna, smiling at the thought.

'A nice downright young man,' said Joan, 'very like you. You'd make a good honest pair.'

'There's no chance of that,' Anna assured her. 'I don't like him well enough.'

'Tom Drew will be relieved to hear it,' said Joan, rising to her feet and disposing of her cigarette end.

At this interesting stage of the conversation, two things happened to distract their attention. The bell shrilled, summoning them to the playground in readiness to lead in their charges for the afternoon session; and even more compelling, Miss Enderby, clad again in her neat green suit and dashing hat, could be seen making her way to her car.

Joan clutched Anna's arm.

'D'you know what? I believe Flo's off for her interview. I heard a rumour that there are three on the short list and the appointment's being made today.'

'No one's said a thing,' objected Anna. 'Surely Miss Hobbs would know?'

'Miss Hobbs's lips are sealed until she receives orders from Miss E. to unseal them,' Joan told her. 'But, mark my words, Flo's finest hour is now upon her!'

They watched their headmistress enter the car, arrange her hat, and insert the car key.

'And good luck to the old girl, say I!' continued Joan warmly, her own cares forgotten. 'Let's hope she pulls it off!'

19. Miss Enderby Triumphs

THE staff of Elm Hill School looked in vain next morning for some sign of success or failure from Miss Enderby.

Morning assembly went as smoothly as ever and the headmistress smiled imperturbably at her flock as they walked from the crowded hall to their classrooms.

'Must be hearing by post,' hissed Joan Berry in Anna's ear, as she passed her in the corridor. 'Perhaps it's a close fight!'

It was all most intriguing and Anna was amazed to find how keenly she wanted Miss Enderby to have her hopes fulfilled.

'I'm getting a thorough-going Elm-Hillite,' she thought amusedly as she settled in her wooden armchair in front of her class.

The suspense was short-lived. At playtime, the next afternoon, Florence Enderby bore into the staff room a large iced sponge-cake, which she placed on the table with a flourish.

'This is something in the nature of a celebration,' she told her expectant staff. 'I want you all to know before anyone else does.'

Her bright gaze swept round the staff room. Her cheeks were pink and she looked unusually handsome. The sapphire ring flashed as she smoothed back her white locks.

'I have been lucky enough to be appointed Head of the new school.'

There was a buzz of congratulation. Everyone was genuinely glad that Miss Enderby had succeeded, and she smiled and nodded her appreciation as the tongues wagged round her.

'The only sad thing,' she went on, when the noise had died down, 'is that I shall have to leave so many of you behind. But I hope, most earnestly, that if you are infants' teachers and would like to continue with me, you will give me your company in the new building. Please think it over. I shall want all the support I can get in this new post.'

Miss Hobbs hurried forward with a knife and Miss Enderby attacked the cake. Someone had raided the kitchen and Anna found herself with the added refinement of a plate for her slice of cake. Normally, the staff were glad enough to balance any such largesse on their saucers, but a plate apiece seemed to emphasize the auspiciousness of this particular occasion.

The post for the junior school, which Miss Enderby would vacate, was advertised in the following week's *Teacher's World* and *The Times Educational Supplement*. A headmaster was to be appointed, the advertisement said, and he would be expected to take up his appointment on 2 September.

'There'll be an ugly rush from half the heads in the area,' prophesied Andy Craig. 'Four-Eyes is making his plans already. I came with him on the bus this morning.'

Four-Eyes, Anna knew, was the ribald name given to a heavily-bespectacled headmaster at a neighbouring school.

'If you mean Mr Forbes,' said Miss Hobbs, primly, 'I doubt if he has a chance. No one's ever forgotten his outburst at the N.U.T. conference.'

'Besides,' said Alan Foster, 'he's no qualifications worth anything. He was my junior at college. And look at his wife!'

Anna thought, with amusement, how parochial school life was under its impersonal veneer. She might have been listening to gossip in her own village. Perhaps, after all, human nature remained much the same, no matter what its environment might be. Would she be any pleasanter as a person if her lot had fallen in better surroundings? The nebulous plans for a country headship one day included a vision of herself as a mellow, wise woman drawing in spiritual refreshment from the natural beauties around her. Would it really be so? Anna found that the more she discovered about people's reactions to their circumstances the more baffling it all became.

'What they want here,' said Alan Foster pontifically, 'is a lively young man in his fifties, say, with plenty of outside interests of a cultural kind – painting, for instance.'

'Or writing,' suggested Andy Craig solemnly. 'Going to apply, Alan?'

'No, no,' said Alan hastily, turning a trifle pink. 'I've too much on hand, in any case. The arithmetic series will take me a few months yet, and I think there's a positive mine for backward children waiting to be tapped. Not,' he added as an afterthought, 'that they'd consider me.'

Almost all the infants' staff had decided to transfer to the new building with their present headmistress. From outside, the school looked almost complete, though the chaos of builders' materials surrounded it still.

Anna had visited it, during the dinner hour, on several occasions, and now she went again with Joan Berry to see where that young lady would be teaching the babies, for Miss Enderby had promised her the reception class as soon as she had heard that Joan would be remaining with her.

The long corridors echoed hollowly. The walls were still of stark grey breeze blocks unadorned as yet with plaster and paint. Wood shavings swirled about their feet in the draughts which eddied from the doorless classrooms, and the cold, antiseptic smell of new wood was everywhere.

The babies' room was in the sunniest corner of the block very near the entrance hall. Joan was delighted with the windows from ceiling to floor on one side and the generous rows of low cupboards which lined the other three sides of her room. Even Anna felt a pang of envy at such wonderful surroundings.

'Well, come too!' urged Joan. 'Infants are much more fun to teach!'

'They'd kill me,' said Anna. 'It's bad enough when they can read a bit – but when they can't even do that – !'

'It's murder while you're at it,' agreed Joan. 'But there's no marking to take home in the evening, and we do end school half an hour earlier.'

'No thanks,' replied Anna firmly. 'I'll stick to the older ones. Besides the new head might be a perfect darling.'

'Better the devil you know than the rogue you don't,' quoted Joan darkly.

They stepped through the french windows on to a terrace. Near by was a paddling pool painted a delectable shade of blue. Banks of earth, later to be grassed, surrounded it, and Anna could imagine it years hence mirroring the flowering shrubs, which were only marks on the architect's plans at this stage. Where would she be then, she wondered? And where would Joan be? Wherever it was, she felt suddenly sure, they would always remain friends.

She linked her arm in Joan's and stepping over a heap of cement-caked planks, the two girls sauntered back happily to their own quarters.

Open Day, as Anna had been warned, now cast its considerable shadow before it. In her innocence, she had imagined that it was simply a normal day in which parents could come to see their children going about their normal business. That a little light refreshment might be made available seemed reasonable enough, when school finished at four o'clock, and that teachers should be willing to discuss their children's work then with interested parents; but Anna had never imagined such preparations for the event. Had all this gone on behind the scenes in her own schooldays, she wondered?

She had spent many a long hour after school mounting work for display and selecting suitable pictures for her walls, but the climax came on the morning of the day itself, when desks were finally tidied, and any superfluous furniture was trundled out to make a little more space for the visitors to circulate in the afternoon.

The noise was deafening. The children were wildly excited

and threw themselves energetically into their labours. Up and down the narrow gangways they raced flinging the debris from their desks into the waste-paper basket, until Anna feared for the safety of her newly hung specimens of work on the walls.

'You are to stay in your seats!' she shouted desperately to her mad charges. 'John will bring the basket round to you. And you are not to snatch the duster from each other like that! I shall choose a sensible, quiet child to dust the desks!'

There was some slight subsidence in the din after this harangue, punctuated by the crashing of books from piles insecurely balanced on seats while their owners busily chased dust, crumbs, pellets of blotting paper, and other desk-trivia through the hole obligingly left in the corners of the desks by the makers for just this purpose. The state of the floor was deplorable but Anna made up her mind to do all the moving first before sweeping up.

'I want four large strong boys to take out these two empty desks,' she said looking round the room. Silence fell, as small chests were thrown out and young backs elongated to make their owners look impressively tough. Anna felt that she was beginning to know her job. Could those psychology lectures at college really be bearing fruit, she wondered?

She chose her henchmen and between them they heaved and hauled the desks through the door and to the end of the corridor. A formidable pile of school furniture was already assembled here, and Tom Drew was trying to put it in some semblance of order. The noise of banging wood was stupendous, and from all the classrooms rose a babel of sound from excited children.

'I'm thinking of taking up pneumatic drilling. More peaceful!' shouted Tom to Anna above the din. She nodded sympathetically before returning to the classroom and her vociferous mob.

The last object to be removed was a large model of a desert

which the children had spent weeks preparing as part of their geography course. It was built in a large square sand tray, borrowed from Joan Berry's room, and was the pride of Anna's class.

Lovingly, they had constructed palm trees from green paper and straight twigs. With infinite patience they replaced them in the oasis, a bed of plasticine, whenever they toppled sideways. Arabs of various shades of brown, according to the plasticine available, had been constructed and dressed in scraps of material brought from home, and squatted by a looking-glass lake which reflected some somewhat misshapen creatures, recognized by the initiated as camels.

It had been a source of infinite interest to the children and the thought of its beauties being hidden from their parents' eyes was almost unbearable. They pleaded pathetically when Anna said that it would simply have to be moved out for the afternoon.

'But, miss, I *told* my mum to look out for it!'

'It's the best thing we've got here!'

'My dad wants to see the Arab wearing his bit of tie!'

Anna felt herself weakening. It was Gabrielle Pugg's tearful remark which made her relent finally, though she knew she would regret it during the visitation.

'I've told my mum all about my camel. She knows I call him "Charlie".'

Pressure was too great to resist and Anna succumbed. The unwieldy, dusty, much-loved object was allowed to stay, and Anna thought philosophically that parents complaining of barked shins and snagged nylons must blame them upon the eloquent tongues of their offspring.

Comparative order was now restored and Anna was relieved to hear the bell which told them that playtime was at hand. After play, she promised herself, the children would be set some really quiet work to calm them down, and she would put the finishing touches to the room with a few well-chosen flower arrangements. She looked forward to a little calm after the fury of the storm.

Anna, even now, had not yet learned the unpredictability of school life.

She returned to her classroom much refreshed for her brief break and cup of tea. There was still a buzz of chatter going on, but there was a different note to it, which Anna's ear, fast becoming sensitive to the nuances of child-noise *en masse*, was quick to notice.

A knot of children stood by her desk peering down intently at something which Arnold held. It would be Arnold, thought Anna, hastening to investigate.

The children parted to let her approach her chair and Arnold held up his trophy with pride. It was a dead slow-worm.

Country girl though she was, Anna had a natural horror of legless things, such as snakes, and even harmless worms and humble little legless lizards, such as this, filled her with revulsion, against all the dictates of her cold reasoning. It would never do, however, to let the children think that she was afraid. With commendable promptitude she praised Arnold and quickly took out a plasticine board from the cupboard.

'Put it on here, dear,' she said, quivering inwardly as the end of the dangling creature brushed her hand. 'Then you can take it round to show the others.'

There were some gasps of apprehension from some of the little girls, and squeaks of horror.

'Don't like snakes!'

'It might be poisonous!'

'Don't you bring it near me, Arnold!'

'Nonsense!' said Anna bravely. 'This is a harmless little animal. It isn't a snake, in any case, and if it were you shouldn't feel frightened of it.'

What a hypocrite I am, thought Anna! She tried to look

with brisk efficiency at Arnold's treasure, coiled in an unlovely loop across the plasticine board.

'Where did you find it?' she asked.

'One of the workmen found it, miss. It was curled up in some sand. He said: " 'Ere, kid, get your teacher to learn you about this!" So I brought it in.'

'It was very kind of him,' said Anna mendaciously.

Arnold, having arranged the slow-worm artistically, stood back to admire it. He smelt his hands interestedly.

'I smells awful,' he remarked, smiling proudly. Anna's distaste for the slow-worm grew, but she put a determinedly bright smile upon her lips.

'Run and wash them, and I'll take it round,' she said, screwing her courage to the sticking place. She looked round her class, putting off the evil moment.

'I shan't think of coming until I see straight backs,' said Anna firmly. The children arranged their bodies in more orthodox form, with unusual swiftness.

'This is a slow-worm,' said Anna, 'that Arnold has brought in. It is really a lizard without legs. It is absolutely harmless and if you ever see one alive you must not harm it. Slow-worms do a great deal of good.'

She paused impressively, partly to add emphasis to her short homily, but mainly to gain strength to pick up the body. It really did smell peculiar, she thought, as she reached towards it, and the sooner it was decently buried the better.

Fighting down her disgust she lifted the board. The slow-worm joggled in the most horrifyingly life-like way as she took it to the front of the class. Gabrielle Pugg backed away nervously.

'I don't want to see it, please miss,' she gasped hastily.

'There's *nothing*, absolutely *nothing*, to be frightened of,' protested Anna advancing.

At this point the slow-worm rolled, in sickening slow motion, over the edge of the board and slid down the length of Anna's frock to the floor. Stifling a scream, and frozen to the spot with horror, Anna heard the revolting plop as it hit the boards.

It was as much as she could do to look down at it, and to pick it up was beyond her. Luckily, a cheerful little boy, whose nerves presumably had been removed, leapt to his feet, scooped up the odorous corpse and dumped it with loving care upon its bier again.

Anna backed away hastily and tried to control her trembling voice.

'Thank you, John. Would you like to carry it round?'

'*Please!*' said the child, with fervour. His eyes shone as he bore it carefully up and down the aisles, and Anna, still shuddering, was able to lean against the furthest cupboard and recover.

As soon as was decently possible, the corpse was put into a paper-bag shroud. and John was entrusted with its immediate burial in the school garden.

Anna watched its departure with relief, opened all the windows, sprinkled a little eau-de-Cologne on her handkerchief and mopped her brow.

'Now, children,' she said, returning to her duties, 'you can all draw a picture of the slow-worm and write a few sentences about it. The best ones can go on the wall for your parents to see this afternoon.'

They set to with a will, and peace reigned again. That pathetic, little, dead wisp of malodorous matter had served a useful purpose after all, thought Anna, watching her children's downbent heads and flying pencils. And all is grist to the mill for teachers.

The afternoon, in contrast. seemed almost leisurely. The parents, many of them known to Anna through the Parent–Teacher Association, were flatteringly pleased with all they saw and complimented Anna on the work shown on the walls and set out on the children's desks. The children were at their most endearing, anxious to show their exercise books to proud fathers and mothers and busily pointing out their own particular contributions to the splendour of the classroom.

'See that fish? No, not that one! The next one – the *good* one! That's mine!'

'Me and Bobby done that picture. Ain't it nice?'

Mrs Pugg was introduced to Charlie the camel, and Anna was relieved to see how much admired the desert model was. No doubt the parents had followed its progress daily from the first pouring in of sand until the final glory of the looking-glass water had been added. In any case they greeted it like an old friend and did not appear to mind edging their way round its awkward bulk.

Anna's heart warmed to them as they eased their way through the congestion of desks and children. Their delight was spontaneous in their children's excitement, and though they may have felt parental misgivings when confronted by some of the besmeared and inaccurate pages in their offsprings' exercise books, they were indulgent enough to keep them from Anna.

When one or two of them thanked her for her work Anna felt unaccountably humble. She was honest enough to realize that it was the parents of children who would make progress however badly taught who most readily gave her the credit, but it was heart-warming to be praised, and she was grateful.

When it was all over, and only the crumbs on the hall floor and the bruised grass in the garden bore witness to the hundreds who had invaded the premises, Anna, wearily locking her classroom cupboards, looked back upon her first Open Day. It may have meant weeks of work, it may have seemed uncommonly like 'window-dressing', and it certainly showed the school in its best silk rather than its everyday homespun; but, on the whole, she decided, remembering the parents' interested faces, it had been well worth it.

20. The Year's End

THE heat and glare of high summer did nothing to flatter
Elm Hill and Anna found the district at its worst.

Clouds of dust, from the unmade roads and the new concrete of half-made buildings, blew endlessly across the flat
wastes, covering everything with fine grit. The long light
evenings kept the children late at play in their gardens and in
the roads, and Anna could hear their shrill wranglings wherever she went. They swarmed about the hot pavements, many
of them pot-bellied in smelly elastic bathing costumes and
with reeking, slimy feet encased in hot rubber sand-shoes.
Most of them clutched garish-coloured ice-lollipops in their
sticky hands, and it was not surprising that as the long hot
spell continued they grew increasingly fractious and inattentive
in school.

Anna paid a visit to the local swimming bath, but the
crowds in and around the water, the noise, the smell, and the
water itself, which was unpleasantly warm and slightly vis-
cous, filled her with such disgust that she went no more.

Walking back through the paper-strewn streets, dodging
the busy shoppers and their panting dogs, Anna thought
longingly of the fields of home. There the cattle would be
collected in the deep shade of the elm clumps, while the heat
shimmered into blue distance. It would be quiet there; quiet
enough to hear a bee bumbling in and out of the Canterbury
bells in the border, quiet enough to hear the whinny of her
pony two fields away. The house would be drowsing in the
heat, its outside walls warm to touch, but inside the stone-
flagged floors and thick old walls would ensure a haven of
coolness. The very presence of surrounding trees and grass,
breathing out their fragrance into the sunlight, promised

solace from the heat, but here, thought Anna, looking at the flash of chrome and glass reflecting the glare from the tawdry shop fronts, there was no refreshment to be found. Town life might have to be her lot for a year or two, but of one thing she became increasingly conscious. She must make her home in the country. She was as lost here, in this wilderness of bricks and mortar, as any pitiful fish lifted from the water and wilting on the bank.

She had made her way home through the old part of Elm Hill and found herself looking once again through the gates of the vicarage. The garden was as shabby as ever, and now, brown and baked with the drought, presented an even more pathetic front. There was something different about it too, thought Anna, and then realized, with a shock of dismay, that the cedar tree, its only touch of beauty and majesty, had been cut down.

Anna felt the tears sting her eyes as she hurried on. It seemed the last straw. How much loveliness had been destroyed to make this sprawling, modern, formless horror? She remembered the old man's words, so many months ago: 'There used to be lovely beds of white violets. Under all these pavements now, they are!' and she grieved for the piteousness of it all.

The cedar tree had gone. Soon Tom would be gone. Elm Hill, next term, would be a desert indeed.

As the term wore on the building activities became more and more frenzied in the new school. Miss Enderby was a constant visitor, and Anna, from her high window, watched her headmistress entering her new domain and surveying its growing beauties, several times a day. Despite the heat, Florence Enderby appeared tireless. It seemed as though this new project had given her added zest. Her spirits were high, her smile radiant, and her staff basked in the balmy atmosphere. Now that her hopes were fulfilled and her energies directed towards this long-awaited venture, Miss Enderby's tension relaxed. It certainly made the last few weeks of a gruelling term very much pleasanter.

The new headmaster had been appointed. His name, they learnt, was Charles Willoughby, and he came from a headship in Northumberland.

'Another foreigner from the Frozen North,' said Andy Craig. 'Beats me why they all flock south when you hear from their own lips how much better everything's done up there!'

'It's sheer altruism,' said Joan Berry. 'They like to give us the benefit of their good luck.'

'It might have been Four-Eyes, don't forget,' said someone else warningly. 'At least we've been spared that.'

'Forbes would have been an excellent choice,' said Alan Foster primly. 'A good sound chap. He was thought a lot of at college, I remember.'

Anna could not help being amused at this complete *volte-face*. Last time poor Four-Eyes had been suggested, she remembered, Alan Foster's scorn had been withering.

'Mr Willoughby's coming to see the school next week,' said Miss Hobbs. 'He's putting up at The Feathers for the night. I met the landlord's wife at Choral practice last night.'

Anna felt warmed by such domestic details. She might have been back in the village, she thought happily.

'Well, I hope he brings his Keatings with him,' said Andy Craig slanderously.

Miss Hobbs raised her eyebrows significantly at Anna to show how much she deplored such vulgarity in the staff room. Andy Craig remained cheerfully impervious to this well-bred hint and rattled on.

'Poor chap! We'll have to show him round a bit. Can't have him thinking that that little flea-club is the best the south can offer. Wonder where he'll live when he moves down here?'

'If he has any sense,' said Miss Hobbs pointedly, 'he'll find somewhere at a distance from the school. And the staff!'

'Good luck to him anyway,' said Andy Craig, tossing down the dregs of his tea cup and wiping his luxuriant moustache with a gaudy silk handkerchief. 'He'll need all the northern pluck he's got to take on Elm Hill!'

One particularly hot afternoon, towards the end of term, Joan invited Anna to tea in her garden.

'The rest of the house is empty,' she said. 'Everyone's holidaying, lucky wretches. I'm monarch of all I survey, at the moment, and that includes a nice cool summer-house.'

It was wonderful, after the hot streets, to sit in the green shade of a matured garden and to see the sunshine filtered through the kindly screen of thick leaves. Here the bees hummed among the lime flowers, and a linnet sang from a rose bush, so that Anna might almost think she was at home. She stretched out luxuriously in the deck chair and listened to the last chapter in Maurice's brief history.

'He'd taken the money. He admitted it,' said Joan lazily. 'Not that he was contrite, of course; just simply hopping mad that I'd found out. Anyway, he said he was going to stay at dear Sandra's house, so I was spared the pain of evicting him.'

'Sandra!' commented Anna. 'It would be something like that! Is she likely to be taken in?'

'She *understands* him, dear,' said Joan mockingly. 'He has never really known security, so he tells me. I have been extraordinarily hard-hearted, I was informed, and he considers that I have no finer feelings whatsoever. He reminded me, somewhat tearfully, that I laughed my head off when he fell in the river at Pangbourne. We were both about six then, and according to poor Maurice, I haven't changed a bit!'

'But what infernal cheek!' protested Anna. 'After keeping the little worm all this time. Were you furious with him?'

'Well, no,' admitted Joan. 'I'm afraid I hurt him much more

than that. I laughed till I cried. He flung out of the flat, and I'm relieved to say I haven't seen him since.'

'What about his things?'

'He'd taken most of them to Sandra's already, but I sent his bath-salts and his sleeping-pills on. I must say it's wonderful to have the flat to myself.'

She rose to pack the tea things on the tray.

'Don't let's wash them now,' said Joan, sinking back after her task. 'It's too glorious to go in. Anyway, you're staying to supper and we'll face the shambles after that. I bet you'll have more to eat, even in my feckless *ménage*, than you will at Mrs Flynn's.'

'I can't wait to get to Mrs Armstrong's,' admitted Anna. 'Yesterday I was given one slice of luncheon sausage, cut as thin as paper, two lettuce leaves and half a tomato for my supper. Mrs Flynn said it was amazing how little one needed in this hot weather!'

'Never mind, you'll be home soon,' comforted Joan. 'Tell me your holiday plans.'

'Devon's off this year,' said Anna. 'The cottage roof is being taken off and put back, so we're staying at home and all helping with the harvest. My brothers are both old enough now to drive the tractor. I wondered –' She broke off and looked at Joan's elegant length doubtfully.

'Would you like to come too? Not to drive a tractor, I mean, but to stay?'

Joan sat up quickly.

'There's nothing I'd like more. But wouldn't I be a nuisance at a busy time like that?'

'You'd jolly well be made to help!' Anna assured her. 'My mother would love another pair of hands to cut sandwiches for the men. They take their lunch and tea out and they eat stacks and stacks of food.'

'It sounds heavenly,' said Joan truthfully. 'And I'd love to come.'

'And what's more,' said Anna, becoming quite excited at the prospect, 'Ted will be there.'

'That *quite* settles it, of course,' said Joan with mock gravity. But Anna could see that she was pleased.

Throughout the term Anna had had cause to remember Joan Berry's warning about the impossibility of getting much work done, but she had never quite realized how little would be accomplished in the children's class work.

The Choral Competition, the Verse-Speaking Competition, the School Sports, and Open Day were all behind her now, but the Area Sports still loomed ahead and besides this an endless number of end-of-year chores remained to be done. Anna's record book bore witness to the lagging-behind of lessons. Far too often, for her peace of mind, a prepared piece of work would have to be set aside for such things as running heats or collecting equipment.

End of term class examinations had to be fitted in, and Anna's own records of each child's progress. She found herself staying later and later at school to get her papers marked up, and her reports and marks made up. The sitting-room at Mrs Flynn's had been barred to her ever since she had given in her notice, and the atmosphere was bleaker than before in that unhappy household.

Anna wished that she had had some warning at college of the pressure of events at the end of the school year. Anxious herself about her future prospects as she approached the end of her probationary year, she found herself more and more impatient of interruptions and horrified at the unforeseen extra duties which crowded out almost all new teaching for the last half of the term.

One of her biggest headaches was stock-taking, which involved counting the many sets of books, and other apparatus, stacked in the classroom cupboards. Gabrielle Pugg seemed to be letting in and out a steady stream of her own and other people's children in search of missing property.

'Please have you got any spare *Happy Valley Readers*?'

'Miss Brown's lost six paint brushes. Have you got any?'

'Please did you return those scissors Miss Berry lent you?'

'Have you got a *Lipscombe Book 3* Arithmetic Book?'

A lighter touch was given by one of Tom Drew's boys who entered to say: 'Mr Drew's lost the globe.' Trust Tom, thought Anna, with amusement, to mislay one simple monumental article like the school globe! It reappeared finally, and inexplicably, in the caretaker's cupboard inside a new pail.

Added to Anna's labours, at this time, was the collecting of money for various things. The children not only paid for small objects which they had made in needlework or handwork lessons, but they had also been asked to contribute something towards a bouquet for Miss Enderby, as she was now to leave the juniors behind. Anna's desk drawer was ajingle with tobacco tins, supplied by Tom, each bearing its quota of money. She only hoped that in the press of events she had put the right amounts into the right tins.

It was almost a relief to get out of the chaos of her classroom to attend the Area Sports. This was to be the last out-of-school activity of the term, and Anna was heartily glad.

It was held in a large stadium about six miles from Elm Hill and the competitors were taken by bus. Anna had the onerous job of marshalling the children for each race and was nearly driven mad by absentees who had to be fetched from refreshment tents, lavatories, and distant portions of the vast stadium, in the very nick of time.

Tom Drew had an even less enviable post as Third Judge, which demanded a keen eye to see which competitor arrived in third place in each race.

'Don't you ever have doubts?' asked Anna when they met during the lunch break.

'Frequently,' said Tom, 'but I stick like glue to my decision. There'd be warfare otherwise.'

It was one of the most exhausting of Anna's teaching experiences, and the fact that the track was a cinder one added to the day's difficulties.

Black-faced, and with grit in her hair, eyes, and clothes, Anna returned to Mrs Flynn's bath, ('Extra, of course,' came the echo, as she turned on the tap), and thanked her stars that another whole year would have to lapse before she need face Area Sports Day again.

On the last evening before Elm Hill School broke up, Tom came to Mrs Flynn's to help Anna collect her belongings and transfer them to his own lodgings.

It was the first time that he had met that redoubtable lady face to face, and Anna was amused to notice the alarm with which he observed Mrs Flynn's tight-lipped smile and cold bony handshake.

She accompanied them upstairs and hovered on the tiny landing as they collected the cases and books, whether for the sake of propriety or because she suspected that Tom might purloin some of her own belongings, Anna could not be quite sure. Her manner had grown increasingly off-hand as the last few hours of Anna's tenancy ran out.

'I'm sure she's been made as comfortable here as my own child,' she observed acidly, watching Tom negotiate the narrow stairs with Anna's suitcase. 'Mind the wallpaper, please. We don't want the expense of repapering *everywhere*. As it is, this bedroom will have to be done out, of course!'

She spoke as though Anna had spent her time throwing soup at her bedroom walls and stamping mud into the flimsy mat on the floor. Anna, for her part, heartily wished that she had. At least the miserable creature would have had some just cause for whining then!

Anna followed Tom into the car, and heaved a sigh of relief as Mrs Flynn slammed the front door shut at the third attempt.

Despite the long hot spell all Mrs Flynn's doors remained obstinate.

'What a wicked old hay-bag!' said Tom, incensed. 'How you've stuck her all this time, I don't know! I should have hanged her from her own miserable banisters in the first week.'

'I didn't think they'd stand the strain,' said Anna candidly.

The contrast between her old quarters and the new delighted her. Tom's bedroom overlooked the leafy garden and was placed above the drawing-room where Anna had first had tea. It was a large square room, warmly carpeted and having two large cupboards, one of which, Anna noticed with approval, housed the hot water tank.

'You'll be pretty snug in the winter,' said Tom, following her gaze. 'Apart from some internal rumblings about two in the morning that old tank's very good company. I shall miss it!'

His trunk lay strapped at the foot of the bed, flanked by boxes and several grips containing the flotsam and jetsam of his time with Mrs Armstrong. Downstairs, in the little room which had been set apart for him and was now to be Anna's, stood piles of books, his gramophone, various bats, racquets, and a hockey stick.

'I'll pack the car up tonight,' he told Anna, 'so that I can flee from Elm Hill as soon as possible tomorrow.'

Mrs Armstrong was as hospitable as ever, despite her sadness at Tom's departure.

'He's a dear boy,' she told Anna repeatedly. 'A dear boy! I can't tell you how I shall miss him. It is such a comfort to me to know you are coming instead. And of course he'll come back *very often* to see you.'

Tom drove Anna back and stopped the car by Mrs Flynn's fast-expiring lilac tree.

'Dear old Mrs Armstrong!' said Tom. 'She's quite right, you know. I told you myself that I'd be coming back, didn't I?'

'You did indeed,' answered Anna. She put her hand on the door-handle, but Tom covered it with his own.

'But can I come and see you before that?' asked Tom. 'Can I come and see you at home?'

'Of course,' cried Anna.

'Often?'

'As often as you like,' Anna promised.

The last day of term was the breathless joyous time it always is, compounded of cheerful good wishes, hurried farewells, and general excitement.

Miss Enderby's bouquet of pink carnations was so large that two children were needed to bear it up the platform steps to present it to her, amidst thunderous applause, at morning assembly. She made a gracious little speech of thanks, and Anna felt quite sorry that she would not be returning to her care next term.

She had been a fine person to start work with, Anna thought, despite her oddities. She remembered the rout of Mrs Bond, the care she had taken to supervise her own first teaching steps, and her ready generosity to all the members of the staff. As Joan Berry had shown her, such trifling conceits as the sapphire ring and the insistence on somewhat archaic courtesies from the children could be readily forgiven in the light of such overwhelming virtues in a headmistress.

She looked round the hall at the staff and realized suddenly how much they had coloured her life in this last bewildering year. Each one had contributed something to her experience of human nature, and had made her, she hoped, more tolerant, and less of the prig she certainly had been.

She felt a sudden wave of affection for portly Alan Foster, still clapping politely at the conclusion of his headmistress's speech, but doubtless thinking of the next book with which to dazzle the educational world; and for Andy Craig, busily tightening the wrist-strap which would be for ever his talisman, the outward symbol of the hero-Andy he might have been.

Her gaze passed on to Joan and Tom to whom her debt was greatest. Not just for one year, but for many, she hoped humbly, would their lives be interwoven with her own.

As for the children, that excitable seething mob of hundreds, now raising the roof with three ear-splitting cheers for Miss Enderby, called for by Miss Hobbs, Anna guessed that they would remain the same dear, devilish, delicious, disarming, infuriating, and exhausting creatures wherever she met them and however long she taught. Somehow, the discovery filled her with surprising contentment.

Next morning Anna lay in the bath under the massive beams of the farm bathroom. The water was twice as deep and twice as hot as ever it was in Mrs Flynn's white-tiled cell.

The thought that she would never set foot again in that miserable establishment was enough to raise Anna's spirits; the added joy of seven weeks at home, far from Elm Hill and its inhabitants, was enough to set her singing. The smell of eggs and bacon cooking in the kitchen below began to mingle with the fragrance of the soapy water. Life was perfect!

She lay back savouring the glory of the moment. Above her, vast bright clouds of steam billowed in the morning sunshine. Outside she could hear her father talking to Ted in the yard, and in the background the voices of birds and animals rejoicing in the bounty of high summer. It was good to lie there drawing in all the pleasures of the present.

And what of the future? To Anna, wallowing gently, sluicing the water over her shoulders, and glorying in the warmth of the sun on her bare back, it all seemed as bright and nebulous as the silver steam above her. Somewhere, sometime, in the misty future, there might be a country school, a little house of her own set in quiet fields, and friends like Joan and Ted – and Tom. Of course Tom would be there.

Meanwhile it was enough to be young, to be hungry, and to be on holiday. She sprang up from the water, in a shower of silver drops, ready to face the bright day ahead.

FOR THE BEST IN PAPERBACKS, LOOK FOR THE 🐧

In every corner of the world, on every subject under the sun, Penguin represents quality and variety – the very best in publishing today.

For complete information about books available from Penguin – including Puffins, Penguin Classics and Arkana – and how to order them, write to us at the appropriate address below. Please note that for copyright reasons the selection of books varies from country to country.

In the United Kingdom: Please write to *Dept E.P., Penguin Books Ltd, Harmondsworth, Middlesex, UB7 0DA.*

If you have any difficulty in obtaining a title, please send your order with the correct money, plus ten per cent for postage and packaging, to *PO Box No 11, West Drayton, Middlesex*

In the United States: Please write to *Dept BA, Penguin, 299 Murray Hill Parkway, East Rutherford, New Jersey 07073*

In Canada: Please write to *Penguin Books Canada Ltd, 2801 John Street, Markham, Ontario L3R 1B4*

In Australia: Please write to the *Marketing Department, Penguin Books Australia Ltd, P.O. Box 257, Ringwood, Victoria 3134*

In New Zealand: Please write to the *Marketing Department, Penguin Books (NZ) Ltd, Private Bag, Takapuna, Auckland 9*

In India: Please write to *Penguin Overseas Ltd, 706 Eros Apartments, 56 Nehru Place, New Delhi, 110019*

In the Netherlands: Please write to *Penguin Books Nederland B.V., Postbus 195, NL–1380AD Weesp*

In West Germany: Please write to *Penguin Books Ltd, Friedrichstrasse 10–12, D–6000 Frankfurt/Main 1*

In Spain: Please write to *Longman Penguin España, Calle San Nicolas 15, E–28013 Madrid*

In Italy: Please write to *Penguin Italia s.r.l., Via Como 4, I-20096 Pioltello (Milano)*

In France: Please write to *Penguin Books Ltd, 39 Rue de Montmorency, F-75003 Paris*

In Japan: Please write to *Longman Penguin Japan Co Ltd, Yamaguchi Building, 2–12–9 Kanda Jimbocho, Chiyoda-Ku, Tokyo 101*

FOR THE BEST IN PAPERBACKS, LOOK FOR THE 🐧

A CHOICE OF PENGUIN FICTION

The Captain and the Enemy   Graham Greene

The Captain always maintained that he won Jim from his father at a game of backgammon ... 'It is good to find the best living writer ... still in such first-rate form' – Francis King in the *Spectator*

The Book and the Brotherhood   Iris Murdoch

'Why should we go on supporting a book which we detest?' Rose Curtland asks. 'The brotherhood of Western intellectuals versus the book of history,' Jenkin Riderhood suggests. 'A thoroughly gripping, stimulating and challenging fiction' – *The Times*

The Image and Other Stories   Isaac Bashevis Singer

'These touching, humorous, beautifully executed stories are the work of a true artist' – *Daily Telegraph*. 'Singer's robust new collection of tales shows a wise teacher at his best' – *Mail on Sunday*

The Enigma of Arrival   V. S. Naipaul

'For sheer abundance of talent, there can hardly be a writer alive who surpasses V. S. Naipaul. Whatever we want in a novelist is to be found in his books' – Irving Howe in *The New York Times Book Review*

Earthly Powers   Anthony Burgess

Anthony Burgess's masterpiece: an enthralling, epic narrative spanning six decades and spotlighting some of the most vivid events and characters of our time. 'Enormous imagination and vitality ... a huge book in every way' – Bernard Levin in the *Sunday Times*